Molly Miranda

THIEF

FOR HIRE

Jillianne Hamilton

TFP

Molly Miranda: Thief for Hire
By Jillianne Hamilton

www.Jillianne-Hamilton.com
www.TomfooleryPress.com

ISBN: 978-0-9939870-2-1

Published in 2015 by Tomfoolery Press and Jillianne Hamilton

For Colby. You are amazing.

For my parents, Mike and Kim, for putting up with me and doing so much for me.

Thanks to Grandma Patsy for always being my #1 fan.

Thanks to Smith Family Farms for their incredible generosity and support.

CHAPTER ONE

I kept my back to the wall, making sure my whole form was in the shadows. A museum employee switched a light on in the next room and rummaged in a metal locker.

What the hell are you even doing back here? Can't you see I'm working?

I forced myself to stay absolutely still and take short, silent breaths. Moisture gathered in my leather gloves. So gross.

Waiting until after *the assignment to eat supper was a stupid choice. I'm hungry. If my stomach grumbles, I'm finished.*

The employee in the next room started humming and my heart rate slowed slightly. Generally, people who hum don't suspect a professional thief is in the next room.

Why is this wig so damn itchy? I can't scratch my neck right now. Must. Not. Scratch. What are you doing in there anyway? Go the fuck home already.

I was in the room next to the locker room—an

examination room where curators might inspect and prepare items before putting them on display to the public. Glassed-in cabinets lined the walls and two long tables stood in the middle. I just hoped she didn't need anything in one of those cabinets or she'd see me for sure.

The locker door shut with a clang and I heard the employee zip up her jacket. Only a wall stood between us. My throat was dry but I couldn't clear it.

Instead of leaving, the employee moved to the exam room doorway, ten feet away from my hiding spot in the corner. I watched her and held my breath.

I readied myself to make a run for it. But where? She'd see me, scream and then call the fuzz.

This assignment offered a substantial payday but it wasn't worth getting caught and going to prison for.

She faced straight ahead to one of the windows across the room. Raindrops made a *clink, clink* sound as they hit the old, thick glass. The glow from outside filtered in through that window, stretching across the floor and ending in a pool of light a few inches in front of my sneakers. The employee yawned, stretching her arms over her head. I stayed frozen.

And that's when I heard it.

"Boom, girl! I like it when yo booty go ooh, ooh, ooh! I wanna slap dat ass, 'cuz you know I like it, girl. Ooh, ooh, ooh—"

She fished her phone from her pocket and went back to the other room.

"Yeah, hi," she said. "I'll be right there. I left my iPod at work. Cool. Bye."

She rushed out, the heavy security door shutting behind her.

I rested my head against the wall behind me, my chest heaving with every loud breath. That was close. Too close.

Having as much information as possible is key when going into an assignment. For instance, I knew this museum had security cameras lining the front and in every room the public can visit. The "Employees Only" areas—like the examination room, the staff room and the basement— were camera-free. The museum also didn't have a single security guard—not uncommon for a museum this size.

I slid out from the shadows and approached the thick metal door at the other end of the room. A panel of numbers was mounted on the wall beside the door.

No one had said anything about a number panel.

I'd seen these security panels before, usually in smaller museums like this one that couldn't afford a full state-of-the-art system. They usually required a four-digit code, and every employee would use the same one. But I didn't know what that might be.

I shrugged and punched in 1, 2, 3 and 4. It beeped, a green light blinked and the door unlocked. I smiled.

People and their passwords.

I turned on my mini flashlight and slowly made my way downstairs. The basement walls were made of old brick, dotted by dark stains where water had leaked in over the years. Dusty crates and boxes were piled in the corners, and four rows of metal lockers stood in the middle of the room. Each locker was labeled with an ID number on a small metal plaque, a tiny keyhole below it. I aimed my flashlight at the lockers, eventually finding #38.

I got my kit from one of my inside coat pockets and

kneeled down, holding my flashlight in my teeth and aiming it towards the keyhole. I inserted my tension wrench and then went to work with my pick, listening carefully for clicks.

Some thieves would choose not to pick the lock, instead just breaking into the locker by destroying the door completely. But then the item inside might get damaged. Even worse, someone would realize the locker had been broken into and evidence might be found easier. But if I picked the lock and then shut the door again, the missing item might not be noticed for weeks or months.

After a few minutes of wiggling the pick in the lock, I heard the final click and pulled the door open.

A plastic bag with a faded blue ribbon lay inside. Specks of dust swirled in the locker around it, dancing in the glow from my flashlight. I put my tools away and carefully slid the bag out of the locker. A card was attached.

#7844 - circa 1780

I raised my eyebrows. The ribbon was tied into a bow and looked like it might turn into a small pile of blue dust at any moment.

I surveyed the other lockers. They certainly held similar treasures and would have similar locks. I could've easily taken a few more items and then fenced them once I was back in the United States.

Don't be stupid. That's how people get caught—by getting greedy.

I tucked the bag carefully into my jacket pocket and shut the door. Quickly and quietly, I made my exit from the museum.

* * *

I met with Audrey at a café in Chelsea. As usual, she was there before me, typing away on her iPhone. She nodded as I sat down across from her.

This place had to be the whitest place in London. Milk-white walls, wooden tables and chairs painted white, and a white wooden counter. Even the pastries were limited to vanilla, almond and coconut. Plus, all of its patrons appeared to be rich white women sipping tea from white china cups. I bet all hell would break loose if someone ever spilled a glass of bright red cranberry juice in here.

Audrey blended into her surroundings like a chameleon. Her crisp white blouse and black high-waisted pencil skirt reeked of designer. Her black Chanel bag sat on the third chair, like it too was taking part in this meeting.

She glanced at my outfit. Audrey had specifically told me *not* to wear denim or leather pants whenever we met. Like I even *own* leather pants!

While Audrey's blonde hair was sleek and pulled back into a low ponytail, my short platinum blonde hair was a matted mess under my wig. I'd plastered on some eyeshadow that morning but probably looked more like a kid playing with her mom's makeup than a young lady who belonged in a café like this one.

A waitress came by and slid a tiny teacup onto our table. I smiled at her while Audrey kept typing away on her phone. I bet she paid more for the case on her phone than most people pay for two weeks of groceries. She eventually put it away and took a quick glance at the smudge of mud on the hem of my jeans. Her nose twitched.

"Good morning, Betty." She didn't smile as she spoke.

"Lovely to see you."

That's me. I'm Betty—at work, anyway.

Audrey has one of those British accents that says, "I'm educated and I come from old money. How do you do? Please don't touch the furniture. It's not meant for sitting upon." I assume her father is Something Something Something the Third. It's also hard to tell when she is being sarcastic and when she's serious. I actually know very little about Audrey. I'm almost certain "Audrey" isn't her real name, though, just like "Betty" isn't mine.

She glanced at my purse as I placed it beside her Chanel bag. She twitched as the two bags touched, like hers might catch herpes or something from mine.

"I take it everything went as planned."

I shrugged. "It was fine." In a single motion, I moved the plastic-encased ribbon from my bag to hers. "Seems like a lot of work for a stupid little—"

Audrey shot me a look then glanced around carefully. "Georgiana Cavendish," she said, almost whispering. "It was a bracelet that actually belonged to her."

I'd never seen her impressed with anything, especially something like an old ribbon that belonged to a dead lady. Maybe Audrey was the client on this one and not just the middleman—or, rather, middlewoman.

"Of course. It's quite an item. Who wouldn't want something like that?" I smiled.

The name sounded only vaguely familiar. I made a mental note to Google it later.

I think she might be a pro tennis player. British people love tennis, right?

I eyed the treats behind the glass counter. "Are the pastries any good?"

Audrey's lips tightened. "I don't eat sweets." She lifted her tea to her lips and gingerly took a dainty sip without making any audible slurping noise. "And neither should you. I don't employ fat people."

I sat back in my chair and looked around the café. None of the other patrons were partaking of the pastries. No cheesecake, no cupcakes, no cookies, no nothing.

What is wrong with all these people?

Audrey stood up. "You'll hear from me soon. Ciao."

I lifted my hand to wave back but she was already out the door.

The waitress at the next table blinked dumbly, looking from the door to me. "She didn't pay for her tea. Can I bring you the bill?"

That sneaky bitch.

"Not yet," I mumbled. "Can you bring me the biggest piece of cheesecake you have?"

* * *

Later that day, ten thousand British pounds were sent to my offshore bank account. I was at Heathrow waiting for my flight home when I got the email notifying me of the transaction.

Airports seem to be the bane of my existence. I visit them frequently and despise them. The waiting. The sitting. The other travelers.

Out of boredom, I took out my phone and Googled

the name Audrey mentioned—Georgiana Cavendish of ... something.

Duchess of Devonshire. Fashionista of the 18th century.

All of the portraits online depicted her as a beautiful lady with a tall mountain of curls on her head. Her elaborate costumes were covered in ribbons, feathers, beading and bows.

If I can make decent money from a single ribbon, just think how much someone would pay for an entire gown.

My heart jumped at the thought.

I wondered how much Audrey made on that assignment. Probably more than me, even though I did all the heavy lifting.

Her only job was connecting a client—that is, someone wanting something valuable—with a hired professional. Me.

My phone buzzed.

To: bettybruce
From: audreyfox
Subject: Re: new assignment
I'll have another assignment available in two weeks. Are you available?

To: audreyfox
From: bettybruce
Subject: Re: new assignment
Aye aye, cap'n.

To: bettybruce
From: audreyfox
Subject: Re: new assignment
What?

To: audreyfox
From: bettybruce
Subject: Re: new assignment
Sorry. Yes, I am available.

* * *

I slid down in my seat and stared out the window as the wing of the plane slid through a layer of fluffy clouds. That was always my favorite part—going above the clouds. It was like looking at the world upside down.

The passenger next to me, a middle-aged woman whose layers of jackets and sweaters overflowed into my seat, gripped the armrests until her knuckles turned white. She glanced at me.

"I hate flying."

"I can tell."

"You must fly more than I do," she said.

I really need to start buying all the seats around me so I don't have to deal with this shit.

"I was just in London visiting my son. He lives there with his girlfriend. They met online. Isn't that neat?" She smiled wide.

I nodded. "Wow."

Are my headphones in my carry-on bag or my purse? Hell, they're in the carry-on. I can't get them unless Chatty Cathy gets up.

"Yeah, he's such a hoot. We went to see all the sights around the city." She laughed. "That Big Ben! Now *that* is a big clock!"

"Bell."

"What?"

"Big Ben is the bell inside the clock."

Chatty Cathy stared at me. "Are you sure?"

Maybe a flight attendant would move me to a different seat if I just slipped them a hundred pounds.

The seatbelt sign blinked off and I practically jumped out of my seat. "I have to pee."

I stayed in the tiny bathroom for a few minutes, just leaning against the wall and staring at the ceiling. It wasn't the most pleasant-smelling place to hide out in.

How many people have had sex in here? It's so cramped in here. How do people even do that?

I frowned at my reflection in the dimly lit mirror and adjusted my shoulder-length brown wig, finger-combing parts of it that looked a bit disheveled. I couldn't wait to be rid of it.

Switching seats would attract unwanted attention. I couldn't do that. Blending in is one of the most important things to remember in my job. Drawing notice gets me into trouble.

I returned to my row, retrieved my headphones from my bag and slid past Chatty Cathy's knees. They poked my ass but I'd rather that than get kneed in the crotch. She smiled up at me and went back to reading the terrible in-flight magazine. Before she could start talking again, I put music on and closed my eyes.

Chatty Cathy tapped my shoulder rapidly to wake me up when our in-flight meal arrived. I peeled the top layer from the steaming food tray.

Clearing her throat, Cathy smiled weakly. Deep creases formed at the corners of her wincing face.

I switched my music off. "Yes?"

She handed me a compact mirror and, trying to be subtle, pointed at my hair.

Shit. The wig.

I slid down in my seat and straightened it. It wasn't as bad as it could've been, just a bit crooked.

"My sister just finished chemo so I know all about it," she whispered, giving my shoulder a light squeeze.

I put her mirror on her tray and started eating. I didn't know what to say.

"Have you had any nausea?"

"I haven't even eaten yet." I looked at my in-flight meal with a mixture of fear and disgust. "I'll let you know."

She smiled. "I meant from the chemo." Her eyes were getting teary.

Oh jeez.

I shrugged. It was better to say nothing in this situation.

At least Chatty Cathy was a little less chatty when she thought I was dying. She even did me a favor when evening approached.

"My friend here," she said, poking a flight attendant in the side as she passed. "She's a bit chilly. Think she could have an extra blanket?"

I have a feeling she wouldn't have been so nice if she knew I was a professional thief and not a cancer patient.

CHAPTER TWO

I was totally beat when I got out of the cab in front of my building on the Upper East Side, just two blocks from the south end of Central Park.

Every woman's home is her castle. My little castle was equipped with a doorman, marble floors in the lobby and an elevator. Bill was working the night shift and greeted me with a smile as I rolled my luggage behind me.

I know what you're thinking—not a lot of millennials can afford a home with a view of the park. I *know* having such fancy digs is not the best way to blend in. I just fell in love when I was apartment hunting and grabbed it before someone else did. The apartment was meant for *me*.

When my mom and stepdad saw the apartment for the first time, I told them I rent monthly, that people exaggerate New York's real estate market—they really don't, it's brutal—and that Dad helps me with rent. I also told them the apartment is haunted, so I got a really good deal. I don't know if they believed me or not. They also had no reason to think I'm a personal assistant who works in an office but they seem to believe that too.

When anyone else asks what I do for a living, I tell them my parents own a ski resort in Vermont and they bought the apartment for me. Thankfully, I'm a private person so I haven't had to explain often.

One of the few people who asked me about this was Nathan Bryant, who evidently bought my story because he moved in with me shortly after. That was six months ago.

I let myself in as quietly as I could but my sneakers squeaked on the wood floor. I left my suitcase in the hall, slipped off my shoes and crept to Nate's open doorway. It was the middle of the night and he was asleep at his desk, snoring softly. His arms were folded under his head, resting on a stack of drawings. The desk lamp's glow shone at the back of his neck. He was still wearing his glasses. A blue colored pencil lay beside his elbow on the desk.

He continued to slumber as I stepped toward him. I picked up a discarded sketch from the floor and smoothed out the creases. The drawing depicted a slender woman in a classic superhero cat suit, a blue cape billowing around her, her full lips curled into a coy smile with one blue eye covered by side-swept bangs. Wind whipped back her pixie cut-style hair, and her tiny nose was dotted with freckles.

Freckles?

Nate snorted and jerked his head up. He removed his glasses and wiped his eyes.

"Hi, Molly." He yawned. "How long have you been standing there?"

"Not long." I flipped the drawing around. "Is this me?"

"That depends. Do you like it?"

"Her boobs are a lot bigger than mine."

"Well, you know how female comic book superheroes are." He smiled shyly.

Oh, that smile. It will ruin me.

"Can I have this?"

"Sure." He stretched. "What time is it?"

"Around midnight. You should probably just go to bed." I turned to leave his room.

"How was Vermont?"

I stared at him for a second.

Vermont. Right. Because I told him I was going to visit my parents.

"It was fine. Go to bed."

Nate set his glasses on his nightstand and started unbuttoning his cotton flannel shirt. He had the most beautiful, perfect collarbone. A tuft of chest hair peeked over the top of his T-shirt. His facial hair grew in thick overnight. He looked nice with facial hair. Really nice, in fact.

He raised his eyebrows at me. "Everything okay?"

"Yeah. I'm just tired. Good night."

Also, you are a beautiful, beautiful man and we should cuddle aggressively.

I fled to my bedroom before he could catch me staring at him some more. I stripped off my jeans, T-shirt and bra and flung my clothes behind me, almost hitting the framed photo of Mom, my sister and I on my bookshelf. I crawled into my unmade king-size bed. If you're going to get a good quality bed and you have the space, you might as well sleep on a king and pile it high with pillows from Barneys and the softest, most expensive bedding Saks Fifth Avenue has to offer. Obviously.

I stared at the bare walls and high ceiling, physically exhausted but wide awake at the same time.

I had been hoping to avoid Nate. And, therefore, avoid awkwardness.

That could have gone worse.

The last interaction we'd had before I took off for the United Kingdom (not Vermont) involved drinking wine, laughing, talking, sharing, making out and falling asleep together on the sofa.

After living in this spacious, beautiful and well-maintained apartment for a year, I had considered getting a cat. Maybe two or five. But I'm not home often enough to keep a pet, and there's only so many conversations you can have with yourself before you think, *I should probably just get a roommate.*

My best friend Ruby mentioned her cousin was looking for a place to live and I tailed him for a few days. I learned about Nate's work, hobbies, personality, criminal record and all the important stuff one needs to know when choosing a roommate.

Yes, I know most people don't *stalk* their potential roommates but I wanted to make sure he wasn't some sort of creep. Although one could argue stalking Nate makes *me* a bit of a creep.

Before I met with Nate to officially interview him and show him the apartment, I thought he was attractive but I didn't expect *feelings* to just show up.

Inviting Nate to live with me was a stupid, stupid mistake. He was just a friend and that was all he could ever be. My life was too complicated for a live-in friend *with* benefits and always would be.

But I ached to go back to his room, crawl into bed with him and snuggle in close.

You can't always get what you want. I think Mick Jagger said that. Or maybe it was Steven Tyler.

* * *

I dreamt my phone was ringing but I couldn't reach it. I was standing in the middle of a busy street in London, forcing traffic to stop for me while I rummaged frantically in my Chanel handbag, which was weird since I didn't actually own a Chanel handbag.

"I'm sorry, I can't find it!" I yelled at the driver of a black cab as he honked at me.

I finally woke up. My phone was ringing for real. I blinked, trying to remember what continent I was on this morning.

I felt around my comforter and found my phone under the pillow. I squinted at the screen, trying to focus my stinging, weary eyes. It was Audrey.

"Good morning," I mumbled.

"You haven't responded to my email yet."

"I'm sorry, what?"

"I emailed you two hours ago," she said. I looked at my watch. It was almost ten. "I'm sorry, did I wake you?"

Her tone swam in a pool of sarcasm. She was not

apologizing for anything.

"I just got home a few hours ago. Can't you just tell me what the damn email said?"

Audrey clucked her tongue. "Tsk, tsk. Do I sense ungratefulness in your voice? I do have others I can go to but I figured you'd want this one."

I paused. She was dangling a tasty treat in front of me, knowing I would jump for it. I hated this game.

"Is this the thing you mentioned yesterday in the email?"

Audrey sighed. "No, this is something a little bigger. I have a new client—an art enthusiast."

I nodded. I'd done several art thefts in the past, especially since switching my focus to United Kingdom assignments. I guess people in North America just don't value art as much as they do 'cross the pond. Usually it's the weirdest paintings. I was once paid a hundred grand to steal a painting called *The Void*. It wasn't a huge canvas—maybe two by two feet—and it was nothing more than a big black square.

Yes, that's right. One hundred thousand bucks for stealing and delivering artwork I could have painted and framed myself for about $15. This job is truly bizarre sometimes.

"My client and her husband divorced a few months ago," Audrey said. "He kept several paintings they commissioned together when they were married. My client would like two specific paintings acquired from his estate."

For those of you just tuning in, "acquired" is Thief Speak for "stolen."

"Do we know how large these paintings are and what kind of security his estate has?" I was wide awake now, sitting up in bed and fully alert. Sometimes getting a call from Audrey is better than coffee.

"I'll email you all the details later today but it looks like one medium and one large canvas. His security looks to be limited to cameras. I'll let you scope out the ex-husband and his home for a few days beforehand."

Inside my head, I was laughing. Educated, well-spoken British women sound ridiculous when they are discussing a felony.

"How much am I getting paid? In American dollars, if you please."

"About five hundred thousand each."

I nodded, smiling wide at my bedroom ceiling.

One million doll—

"For each of you, rather."

Smile gone.

"Pardon?"

"Don't be stupid, Betty. You only have two hands. You cannot retrieve two paintings by yourself. What are you going to do, make two trips?"

I pouted. I felt like screeching, "This is so unfair!" into the phone but I needed to sound like a mature, responsible and capable burglar.

I knew Audrey well enough to know she might just give the job to someone else, and I wasn't stupid enough to let pride get in the way of half a million dollars.

I closed my eyes. "So who, pray tell, will I be working with?"

"Does that matter?"

"Absolutely!" I said. "I'd rather not go to prison because

I'm stuck with an amateur who fucks up and gets us caught."

I pictured Audrey sitting at a minimalist-style desk in a modern and immaculate office, staring into her phone with a look of disgust at my use of the F-bomb.

"Oh, Betty, don't flatter yourself," she said quickly, almost under her breath. "Some might say the same thing about working with you."

Touché.

"Alright," she continued. "Your flight to Aberdeen is in two weeks."

I bit my lip and didn't say anything.

Audrey sighed again. The woman was a factory for exasperated sighs.

"Aberdeen is in Scotland."

I snickered. "I knew that."

I did not know that.

"The estate is an hour outside the city. I'll arrange for a car and lodging for you and your partner. He'll be taking the lead on this one because he has more experience and knows the area. I'll be in touch."

"Taking the lead?" I blurted. "Um, *no*—and you hung up on me. Awesome."

What a warm, personable individual she is.

I'd only been to Scotland once before, on one of my first jobs working with Audrey. She'd sent me to Glasgow to steal a signed football—or *soccer* ball, as I found out later—from a guy's personal collection. It wasn't a high-paying job and it rained the whole time I was there. But at least I got to work alone on that assignment.

It hadn't gone so well when I worked with a partner

once before. I don't even remember her name. She mostly just followed me into a guy's house while I did all the work. She couldn't pick the lock and she couldn't hack into the security system. In the middle of the job, her goddamn phone rang. And she answered it.

"Heyyyyy youuuu!" she squealed into her phone.

My jaw dropped and I prepared to bolt. She saw me staring at her and held her hand over the receiver.

"Do you mind?" she hissed.

I went on with cracking a safe—oh yeah, something else she didn't know how to do. On the way out, she was *thiiiis* close to knocking over a marble bust. She was responding to a text instead of watching where she was going.

I told Paul, my former employer, about her lack of professionalism the next day when I gave him the documents we were sent in to retrieve. I slid them across his desk and folded my arms over my chest.

"She didn't do anything but slow me down. I could've done that job on my own. It was a basic assignment. In fact, I *did* do everything myself! Why the hell did you send her in with me?"

Paul shrugged and reached for the document. I slapped my hand down on it.

"Seriously. It won't happen again. Or I'm done."

He didn't try it again. Instead, he introduced me to Audrey, and soon after I was occasionally working for her on a trial basis. Eventually, she trusted me enough to hire me a few times a month. I didn't need Paul anymore.

I had the place to myself so I pulled on an oversized T-shirt and went hunting for Froot Loops in the kitchen.

I stared out the big window in the living room, chewing lazily. Taxis on the street below looked miniature as they crept along together in a herd. I could see the tops of trees in Central Park. People on the sidewalk looked like ants, scurrying around down there. A view like this made me feel like a queen.

"You're not wearing pants."

I jumped and my cereal bowl and its contents flew into the air. Cold milk splashed onto my bare feet. I whipped my hands in front of my underwear.

Nate laughed his head off.

"You scared the shit out of me!" I yelled as I scurried down the hall to my room. I grabbed some PJ pants. "Aren't you supposed to be at work?"

"I don't go in until three," he said.

When I came out—this time not half-naked—Nate was already cleaning up the mess from my cereal with paper towel.

"Sorry about that." He smiled up at me.

I shrugged. "It's okay. I probably shouldn't be walking around in my underwear anyway."

"No, no. You wear whatever you want." He stood up.

I rinsed the bowl out in the sink and avoided eye contact. It was difficult since he was looking directly at me, still smiling.

"So, what did you do in Vermont?"

"Mom and Joe just got Netflix so we watched some movies." I leaned against the counter. "Ya know. We just kinda ... hung out."

Liar, liar. PJ pants on fire.

Nate was already dressed in dark jeans and a faded blue tee, he had shaved and his chocolate brown hair was neatly styled. I suddenly felt a little silly in my *SpongeBob SquarePants* PJ pants.

"What did you get up to here while I was gone?"

"I had the day off so I went to Connecticut to visit my grandmother. She keeps suggesting I just quit my job and try to make the comic artist thing work." He laughed. "She has no idea how much this city costs."

Nate's day job was waiting tables at a super fancy restaurant in Midtown. Like many creatives in this city, he fantasized of one day leaving that job to pursue his dream job full-time. In Nate's case, this involved drawing and writing comic books. The rich older ladies who dined at the restaurant loved him and tipped him well—so well that leaving would mean a major loss of income. More than once, he said he thought he might be stuck waiting tables forever.

Nate glanced at the bowl in the sink. "Why don't I make us an early lunch? I destroyed your breakfast, after all."

"It was cereal. It's really not a big deal."

"No, really. I was thinking of making eggs anyway." He playfully waved me out of the kitchen. "Come back in twenty minutes."

After a delicious lunch of omelet, toast and orange juice, I sat back in my chair and wiped my mouth on a napkin. I didn't even know we *had* napkins.

I really should learn to cook. Or at least stop depending on delivered pizza and Chinese food so often.

"That was yummy. Thank you."

"So… That thing that happened..." Nate looked at me from behind his coffee mug and took a sip.

I raised my eyebrows at him.

"Are we just going to pretend nothing is going on?"

He knows. Nate knows what I do for a living. He knows I was in England stealing that ribbon. Shiiiit.

I shook my head. "I don't know what to say. It's complicated."

My throat suddenly felt dry. My right hand started to shake so I whipped it under the table, out of sight.

Nate smiled. "It doesn't have to be."

The hell…?

I frowned. "Wait, what are you talking about?"

"What are *you* talking about?"

"I asked you first."

Nate shifted his gaze to his empty plate. "I'm talking about what happened the other night. On the couch."

"Oh!" I burst out laughing, relieved. I stopped and cleared my throat. "Yeah, that's what I meant, too. Of course."

"Okaaaaay… Are we going to talk about it?"

I picked up the empty plates and took them to the sink. "If you want to."

He didn't say anything so I tried to go first.

"Uh, well, you and I … um…" I giggled awkwardly.

Say something, you idiot.

He took my hand and stood closer to me.

He smells like nature. How is that even possible?

"This is really hard to talk about," I whispered.

"I know. It's okay."

Screw it. It's go time.

27

I grabbed the front of his shirt and brought his lips to mine—a little harder than I meant to. Our teeth knocked together.

"Oh, my god, I am *so* sorry!" I yelled, rubbing my mouth.

"That kinda hurt," he said, laughing.

He smiled and touched my cheek. And then we attacked each other like two drunk teenagers on prom night.

I threw my arms around his neck and kissed him again. The dining room chair he was sitting on got knocked over on its side. I somehow got my legs wrapped around his waist and he carried me to the sofa. Nate's hands moved up my torso. I struggled to get my T-shirt off as I straddled his lap.

Stupid sleeves, why are you so difficult sometimes?

I couldn't stop myself. I went for it. What can I say? I've always been kind of a go-getter—just not usually in the sexy sex time way.

"Are you on the pill?" he whispered between kisses to my neck.

My eyes flashed open. "No. Uh, it makes me cry sometimes so I went off it."

Actually, I constantly forgot to take it at the right time because I switch time zones on a regular basis.

I swallowed. "Do you, um, have *condoms*?" I whispered the last word. Why do sexy times become so unsexy when protection is brought up?

Nate kissed me hard on the lips and said, "Mmm-hmm."

I clawed at his T-shirt and pulled it over his head, tossing it aside.

"I've wanted this for so long," Nate whispered, lowering me down onto my back.

"Me too." I smiled up at him.

He struggled to get his pants off, tripped over a pant leg and landed on me, elbow first. Right into my stomach.

I yelped in pain and then laughed as he apologized eight times in a row.

I pointed down the hall. "Maybe we should just go—"

He grabbed my hand and led me to his bedroom.

I wish I could say the sex wasn't awkward. Nate got a leg cramp partway through but recovered quickly, thankfully. I dug my fingernails into his shoulders a little too hard. I banged the back of my head on his night table and there was a lot of sweat and he still had his socks on and my bra was, like, half off. It just wasn't how I'd imagined it.

Not that I had been thinking about sleeping with him or anything. Well, maybe a little.

We both rolled onto our backs and stared at the ceiling.

"Well then. That was fun." Nate struggled to catch his breath. "Really, really good."

I nodded. "Uh-huh." My bare stomach was moist with perspiration. Ew. I pulled a sheet over my torso, suddenly feeling exposed. Too exposed.

Neither of us said anything for a while. What was there to say?

Shit.

* * *

I hid in my room until he left for work that afternoon. I don't think my room has ever been so tidy. I even exercised in there. Anything to avoid directly thinking about what I had just done and all the ways it could ruin a perfectly good roommate relationship.

You are a very stupid woman.

I know.

For serious. What were you thinking?

I wasn't thinking.

Maybe you should get a female roommate next time around. Or maybe you'd end up fucking her, too.

I could keep living with Nate and keep things professional.

Sure you can.

Oh, shut up.

If I continue living with him and things progress, I'm going to have to tell him I'm a burglar for bounty. But perhaps I'm getting ahead of myself. It was just sex. He probably thinks of me as a good friend ... whom he can have slightly uncomfortable sex with sometimes.

Oh, gross. What is happening to me?

* * *

Later that evening, I slid into a bubble bath. The water was just the perfect temperature and Norah Jones sang to me from my iPod. It's funny how comforting a bubble bath can be. All can feel right with the world, even just for a short time.

That is, until your employer calls.

I dried off my hands and fumbled with the phone, trying not to drop it into the bath with me.

"Good lord, Betty. Do you do anything else but sleep?"

"I wasn't sleeping." My jaw clenched. "And I'm fine. How are you?"

"The job in Scotland has been bumped up. The client will be in London for a few days for a conference. Your partner wants to do some prep before that. There's a flight from JKF leaving in three hours. Can you—"

"I'll be there."

Anything to get out of New York for a few days.

CHAPTER THREE

I left a note on the kitchen table for Nate:

Aunt Grace is having emergency gall bladder surgery. Going to Vermont for a few days. Not sure when I'll be back. -M

I don't even have an Aunt Grace, but I figured that was probably better than *Avoiding you by going back to the UK for the second time in a week, this time to steal a painting or two. Ya know, the usual.*

I was lucky enough to sleep for nearly the entire flight to London, my first of two flights that day. I felt like a zombie when I got there. I needed coffee so very, *very* badly.

Heathrow Airport is like a city within a city. Tourists, business travelers and everyone in between all rushing to catch transit and connecting flights. I like it because it's easy to go unnoticed.

I went through customs, finally found a little coffee shop and joined the queue. I was so out of it. I opened my little travel clutch and checked my tickets and passport for the tenth time. I stared off into space.

What the hell am I gonna do about Nate? Was it a one-time thing? Are we going to try to be in a relationship? I can't do relationships. My life is way too complicated for that. This situation is just so totally fu—

I was poked in the back. Hard.

"Jeez, ow!" I whipped my head around.

The man behind me put the tip of his umbrella back down on the floor. He was tall, maybe in his late twenties. He wore a tailored wool suit, obviously expensive—not a speck of dandruff or lint on it. His wavy golden brown hair rested on his shoulders. His goatee was neatly groomed, and one of his perfectly shaped eyebrows arched while he smiled at me.

"Did you just poke me with your umbrella?"

"I did." He grinned.

"Could you maybe, I dunno, *not* do that?" My eyes narrowed. "It's pretty friggin' rude."

"Could you perhaps move ahead in line and order your double espresso mocha latte cappuccino?" he said in an Italian accent. "Or whatever the hell it is you Americans drink."

"Of course," I snapped. "Like Europe doesn't have Starbucks now." I moved ahead in line.

He snickered and threw money on the counter. "Get the lady whatever she likes." He smiled at me. "Take it easy, Molly." And then he disappeared into the crowd.

My heart lurched in my chest. My face felt warm.

The barista stared at me. I gripped the handle of my suitcase to try to stop my hand from trembling.

"Oh, um, I'll have … uh … coffee? Black coffee," I blurted.

Nobody on this side of the Atlantic is supposed to know my name is Molly. Over here I'm Betty Bruce, not Molly. I try to make a point of not introducing myself to people here—not as Betty and especially not as Molly. Who the hell is that guy? How does he know who I am? Where did he go?

Not good.

He saw the real me. No wig and no big dark sunglasses to hide behind. Now I couldn't put on my wig until after the flight, in case I ran into him again. Had I maybe met him before? Did I know him from New York somehow and just wasn't recognizing him?

I checked my watch. I only had twenty minutes before my connecting flight to Aberdeen.

I sat at a table near the café and tapped my foot as I sipped my coffee. This had never happened to me before. I didn't know if I should abandon the mission or call Audrey. I grabbed my phone and called her, just in case. No answer.

Word to the wise: don't glance around frantically and look like a nervous wreck in a big airport. It causes security to keep an eye on you.

I got my sunglasses out of my suitcase and put them on. It made me feel a tiny bit more secure. Also a bit like a celebrity hiding from paparazzi.

I slurped my coffee and checked a nearby clock every thirty seconds. I tried calling Audrey again but there was still no answer. I'd have to go ahead with the assignment.

Maybe I misheard him. Maybe he said "honey" and not "Molly." It's busy and loud in here. I might've just imagined it. In fact, he probably said "honey." Or "Polly." Or "Collie." Yeah, that's it. "Collie." I bet "Collie" is just what Italians call strangers they meet at airports. It probably happens all the time!

The gate for my flight opened. I tossed my coffee and rolled my suitcase down a hall, up an escalator, down an escalator and down another hall. Heathrow is big. Have I mentioned that? I waited to board the next flight with a few other passengers. Thankfully, this flight was fairly quick—about an hour and a half. That was peanuts after flying over the Atlantic twice in three days.

I followed the other passengers on and took my seat. I'd been wise this time and booked a comfortable seat in business class for the trip over to London but hadn't bothered for this one.

We were minutes from takeoff when the empty seat next to me was suddenly filled by none other than the rude Italian in the expensive suit.

I avoided eye contact but could see his Cheshire Cat grin, even from the corner of my eye. He kept smiling directly at me until I gave up and looked back at him.

"Oh," I said, "you again." I wanted to say a lot more than that but was trying to stay calm and not make a scene.

"I bought you coffee. The least you can do is thank me," he said.

"You also poked me with an umbrella."

He lowered his voice. "Now, don't be like that, Molly." This time I knew for sure he said my name. "I meant no harm."

"My name is not Molly," I snapped.

"Of course it isn't." He winked at me, his blue eyes sparkling.

I turned back towards the window.

"We haven't even taken off. There's really not much to see out there yet."

I threw him a glare and grabbed the in-flight magazine. I flipped to an article titled "Ten Can't-Miss Restaurants in Wales" and pretended to be immersed in it. It didn't work.

"My name is Rhys, by the way."

I nodded, still staring at the magazine. "That's nice."

He took out his phone, typed something and handed it to me. I rolled my eyes, tucked the magazine between my thighs and looked at the message.

You should probably know my name if we're going to be working together for a few days.

I looked up at him to see his expression. He smiled and lifted his hand to playfully wave.

No way. This has got to be a fucking joke.

That didn't clear up how he knew my name, what I looked like or why he was being an irritating jackass. Audrey knows me as Betty, and Paul knew me as Betty before that.

I handed his phone back. "Wonderful. Perhaps we can talk about this a little more when we get to Aberdeen."

Rhys shrugged. "Of course."

He spent most of the flight playing Angry Birds on his phone and flirting with flight attendants. He even got a free drink out of it. He was certainly handsome and charming in a James Bond sort of way, but his cocky arrogance was unbearable.

So. This was to be my partner in crime for the biggest burglary assignment I'd ever done. He wasn't exactly trying to blend in. Like, *at all.*

He leaned over and tapped the shoulder of the woman across the aisle. Her shiny, shoulder-length red hair framed a round face. The woman's green eyes lit up when she realized Rhys was about to speak to her.

"I didn't know there was a fashion show happening in Scotland any time soon," he said.

"Excuse me?"

"Oh," he said, blinking dumbly. "I assume you're a model."

The woman giggled and blushed. "No, just visiting some friends," she said in a timid English accent.

"What do you do when you're not visiting friends?"

"I'm an office manager."

"You're joking!" Rhys said. "I don't believe it! You're too beautiful for that!"

The man next to her—obviously her husband or boyfriend—was glaring at him *hard.* I thought he might leap out of his seat and strangle Rhys right there.

I sank further and further into my seat. I've always found comfort in being invisible. If you're not seen, you can't be identified. But sitting next to Casanova was putting me on edge since several sets of eyeballs were aimed in our direction.

We are going to get noticed. Someone will be able to identify us and I'll end up doing jail time because of his stupidity. What was Audrey thinking, pairing me up with this shithead?

The best thing I could do was put on my headphones and pretend not to know him. Once we arrived in Aberdeen, I could easily lose him in a crowd.

Call Audrey and get the location details from her. There is no way I'm going to jeopardize my future because of this guy. No way.

We arrived at Aberdeen International Airport in the middle of the afternoon and I avoided Rhys as much as I could. I didn't want to be associated with him and I definitely didn't want people to think we were traveling together.

He caught up to me. "You're in a rush."

"I have to call Audrey."

"About what?"

I stared at him and glanced at the crowd at the airport. "Something's come up."

"You'll have to call her later. Our car is waiting." His accent switched from Italian to Scottish and the look in his eyes was suddenly serious. "Come with me."

"What the hell?" I whispered. "You're not Italian?"

Rhys smiled at me over his shoulder and winked. "I'm a man of many, many, *many* talents."

This guy was seriously ooky. I followed him out of the airport, dragging my suitcase behind me. "Wait, where's your suitcase?" I said.

"I don't have one." He shrugged and kept walking, quickly but not unusually so for a traveler in an airport.

The change in his accent and mannerisms was unsettling. A knot formed in my stomach as we navigated through the airport and found the car rental place. Rhys was putting my suitcase into the trunk of a black BMW with tinted windows when I was struck by fear.

What if this guy tries to murder me? The police report would say I got right in the car with no struggle so I must have known the suspect.

Well, the report would say that about Betty Bruce, not me, since my work passport and ID cards were in my bag—nothing that would identify me as Molly Miranda.

I still didn't know how Rhys knew my name. I didn't even know for sure if Audrey arranged this.

I took a step back from the car. "I think I'd better call Audrey."

Rhys's eyes narrowed. "What for?" He glanced around to see if anybody was noticing this little exchange. Suddenly *he* was concerned about appearances.

"She asked me to check in when I got to Scotland."

Rhys rolled his eyes. "Fine, fine. But hurry up, we've gotta go."

I ducked into a nearby ladies washroom and away from Rhys. After five rings, she picked up.

"Audrey. It's Betty. I'm at the airport in Aberdeen."

"Wonderful," she said. "Did Rhys meet you in London?"

"Er, yes—"

"Is there a problem?" She sounded annoyed.

"This guy checks out with you? I'm not sure he's trustworthy. He wasn't exactly trying to blend in on the flight—"

"He's professional, he knows the area and he's been doing this longer than you," she snapped. "You could learn a thing or two from him. Now, go do your job."

And then she hung up on me. I really wished she'd stop doing that.

Sometimes I wondered if putting my life in the hands of that woman was a good idea.

I came out of the bathroom and walked towards the car. Rhys, already sitting in the driver's seat, ready to go, raised an eyebrow at me.

"So?"

I crossed my arms over my chest. "If you turn out to be a serial killer and I get stabbed to death, I'm going to be *so* pissed."

We didn't say much until we got out onto the highway.

"So," I said, "are you actually Scottish or is that just a fake accent too?"

He smiled. "Yes, I'm *actually* Scottish. Do you know a lot of Italian men named Rhys? And don't worry. I'm not a murdering psychopath either."

I rolled my eyes. "Some women try to avoid getting into vehicles with men they don't know, especially when they are in a place they've never been."

He opened his mouth to protest, but nothing came out. He frowned instead. "Good point. My apologies." He glanced at me from the corner of his eye. "You're a bit younger than I was expecting. How long have you been doing this sort of work?"

"Long enough. Does it always rain here?"

"Yup."

"Great."

I really need to get Audrey to book an assignment for me in, say, Morocco.

We drove for about an hour, eventually turning off onto a stone driveway and pulling up to a manor that looked about a thousand years old.

"What's this?"

Rhys raised an eyebrow. "It's an inn. We'll be staying here for a couple of days." He glanced out the windows to check for witnesses then reached behind his neck, peeling off a wig. The short, dark hair underneath was slightly disheveled. He ran his hand through it and it fell back into place all by itself. It was kind of magical.

He smiled at me, looking much more professional and less like a poor man's Fabio. "Had you fooled, didn't I?"

I rolled my eyes. "Obviously not. Anyone for miles could tell that was a wig."

Totally didn't realize that was a wig. I should've been able to tell.

He reached across me and popped open the glove box. He tossed the wig inside and got out of the car.

I followed him down a cobbled path and up a set of stone stairs. Rhys opened the heavy medieval-style door and we went inside. Rustic wooden beams crisscrossed the ceiling in the lobby, and light fixtures that looked like candlesticks were mounted on the wood-paneled walls. Classical music played somewhere but was dulled by the rain pounding against the windows. Beautiful Persian rugs lined the floor. I felt bad stepping on them with my wet sneakers.

As we got closer to the reception desk, Rhys grabbed my hand and pulled me tight to his side, shoving a ring into my palm.

"We're a couple," he whispered. "Go along with it. Don't say anything."

Inside, my blood boiled. His *wife!* Yeah, right. My knuckles hurt as I squeezed my fists, fighting the urge to shove him, grab the car key and make a run for it.

I tried to slide the gold band, complete with one monster of a rock mounted on it, onto my ring finger but it was too small. I bit my lip and forced it over my knuckle, squeaking in pain as it pinched my finger.

I'm going to have to cut off that finger.

"Good day. How may I help you?" said an older woman with a gentle Scottish accent who was sitting at the front desk. She had her hands folded in her lap. When she looked up at us, her cheeks glowed pink. She looked like almost every cartoon character of "Grandma" ever drawn.

"This is *some* place y'all got here," Rhys said, slipping effortlessly into a Texas accent—a pretty good one, too. "How old is the building?"

"Well, it's been in my family for generations," she gushed. "First built in the early 1600s. It's been renovated quite a few times since then, though, I assure you." She giggled.

"Wonderful!" He looked around and nodded approvingly. "We'd like to book a room for two days." He wrapped his arm tight around my shoulder, giving me a squeeze. "We're on our honeymoon." He kissed me hard on the cheek.

I forced a weak smile and my nose twitched.

I hope my eyes aren't full of tears right now. They may have to cut off the entire finger. Or it'll just fall off from lack of blood flow. Can a finger just fall off like that? Or would it just shrivel up, die and then just dangle there? Oh gross. Hang in there, finger. We'll get through this.

"Lovely! Our honeymoon suite is available."

"Sounds perfect!" Rhys said before I could interject.

I am going to straight-up kill this man.

* * *

The honeymoon suite was a stone cottage set back from the main inn. The loft had a king-size bed and an en suite bathroom while the first floor had a sofa, TV, fireplace, kitchen area with a table ... and a heart-shaped hot tub.

I glared at it, then at Rhys, and dropped my suitcase.

"You've got to be kidding me. *Why*—"

"Because recently married couples like to shag in hot tubs." Back to the Scottish accent. He opened the fridge. "Complementary bottle of whiskey. Nice."

"Not the hot tub. I was *going* to ask why are we staying *here?*"

"A man and a woman who are *not* a couple staying at a country inn seem suspicious. Remind me to give this place a good review on TripAdvisor."

"We could be here on business."

"If we were here on business, we'd be staying in the city, not out here." He picked up his suitcase and went upstairs. "I'll be down in a few minutes, honey buns."

These games with Rhys were irritating. The seamless accent switch, the wedding ring bullshit. Most importantly, my name just being thrown around.

I turned on the television and considered what it might be like to kill a man. This man, specifically.

Would anyone really miss him? I highly doubt it.

I skimmed the channel menu. Channel surfing in a foreign country is like reading a restaurant menu in a language you don't speak: some of it looks familiar but two thirds of it just looks bizarre. I totally don't get British humor at all. These people are so weird.

I opened my nearby suitcase and picked up the wig I had brought with me: shoulder-length, golden brown. I couldn't wear it around the inn in case the owner saw me.

I tugged at the ring on my finger, spinning it around to

loosen it. I breathed on it to build up sweat to slip it off. It would. Not. Budge.

"Fucking piece of shit," I whispered. "Ow, ow, ow, ow."

My phone buzzed with an incoming text.

Nate: *Just checking in. Everything all right?*

It was nice of him to be concerned, even if it was for a made-up relative. I heard the bathroom door and pocketed my phone.

Rhys came back downstairs, now clean-shaven. He looked like a completely different person than the one I'd met this morning. He was actually handsome. Still an asshole, though.

He rubbed his cheeks and chin. "Glad to be rid of that beard."

"That's why you acted the way you did on the plane," I said. "People will remember an Italian with long hair and facial hair, but not you. Smart."

"'Brilliant,' I believe, is the word you're looking for."

It was time for me to be assertive. "Why did you call me 'Molly' earlier?"

Rhys riffled through his suitcase. "Because that's your name."

"Why do you think that's my name?"

He shrugged. "Audrey told me."

"No, she didn't. She knows me as Betty Bruce. *That's* my name."

Rhys smirked. "Betty Bruce sounds like a superhero name. Also, that's the name on your fake passport, not your real name—"

"No, it's—"

"Your name is Molly Miranda. You live in New York. You own a flat in Manhattan and you live with a *waiter* named Nate." He looked at me. "Is he your boyfriend?"

Damn it.

"We're just friends," I snapped. "And don't say 'waiter' like it's a big deal because I'm from New York. Half the people in New York who are in their twenties work in food service. Nate and I are just—"

"Vermont."

"What?"

"You said you're *from* New York, but you're not. You're from Vermont."

My chest was heaving and my knuckles hurt from squeezing my fists. "How do you know all this stuff about me?"

He crossed his arms over his chest. "Now what kind of professional would I be if I didn't check up on the young ingénue I'd be sharing an assignment with?"

I stared at him. "Go on."

"Audrey told me your name is Betty Bruce. First I hacked into the American passport database and found Betty's passport and acquired your photograph."

Like all passport photos, mine was terrible. I looked like an annoyed zombie.

Rhys spoke quickly and without any hesitation. His Scottish accent wasn't thick enough for me to misunderstand him.

"Betty Bruce doesn't have much of an online identity— no Facebook, Twitter, Instagram, whatever. So, I used the FBI's facial recognition software to cross-reference it with anyone else with an American passport."

I raised my eyebrows. "FBI?"

"Oh yeah. Lovely little program. I made some adaptations to the program myself and made it even better. It's pretty hush-hush, so don't go telling all your friends about it." He grinned and continued. "There was no match there, so I went about searching the crime records for each state using your passport photo. Up comes information on a college student, Molly Miranda, who was charged with breaking and entering. I'm not sure why you would break into your professor's house but that doesn't really matter."

I sat on the edge of the sofa and stared at him, shoving my hands under my thighs to make them stop quivering.

"From there I found your social media accounts and the deed to your flat. Actually, I was able to gain access to information for everyone living in your building. Did you know the person in the flat right below you is an heiress? I would get in there and poke around if I were—"

"Focus, Rhys. Focus."

"Right, of course. Since you haven't had any more brushes with the law, or a *normal* job since college *and* your parents are far from rich, I figure you make a pretty healthy income from doing *this* job." He shrugged. "So I feel pretty good about this partnership."

"He wasn't *my* professor," I blurted out.

"No?"

"Someone paid me to get the exam answer sheet for them." I shrugged weakly.

"And you got caught climbing out of a window by one of the neighbors."

My jaw clenched. "I was there. You don't have to

remind me."

"We'll dig further into your criminal history later on, kid." He checked his watch. "I want to show you something in town. Maybe we should grab a spot of supper while we're there?"

I'd rather kick you repeatedly. But duty calls.

* * *

The mealtime conversation was a little sparse. I'm sure the other restaurant patrons thought we were a couple in the middle of a big fight but trying to have a nice time anyway.

I was exhausted from the two flights and mostly just wanted to get back to the hotel and go to sleep. But Rhys said he had something to show me.

We sat by a big window at the restaurant, watching the rain pouring—still. Scotland seems to be one big soggy nation. Soggy kilts, soggy haggis, soggy bagpipes. Soggy everything.

Near the end of the meal, Rhys pointed to the building across the street.

"See that office up there on the third floor? The one with the chair in the window?"

I nodded.

He sipped his beer. "That's his."

That could only mean one thing—our target.

"How long have you been tailing him?"

"Off and on for two weeks. And I happen to know he's booked a train ticket for tomorrow night and a return ticket on Wednesday afternoon, so we know exactly what times he'll be away from his house."

I forced myself not to be impressed. Then again, after discovering my real identity, finding flight information for a target likely wasn't much of a challenge.

"He's been working late regularly since the divorce, probably because there's no one to go home to anymore." Rhys glanced at me, then back to the window. "Speaking of divorce, where's your father these days?"

"Why?"

"I couldn't find much of anything on him during my research."

Research? Is that what they're calling stalking these days? I suppose I did the exact same thing to Nate... Well, not exactly the same but damn close.

"I haven't seen Dad in years," I said. I hoped he would drop the subject. I looked back at the office. "Do you want to go up there?"

"Already done," Rhys said, putting on his coat and nodding to the door. Time to go. "He keeps a bottle of vodka and a sexy photo of his ex-wife in his desk drawer."

"How sexy we talkin' here?"

Rhys shrugged. "Oh, I'd definitely fuck her."

CHAPTER FOUR

No matter what or who the target, I always wake up feeling pumped on game day. It's that same feeling a kid gets on the first day of summer vacation—the fun is about to begin, the real world seems miles away and there is an ocean of possibilities in between.

Waking up after a full night's sleep in a soft bed doesn't hurt either.

I didn't even have to wake up to an awful alarm. Instead it was to the sound and smell of crackling bacon. I winced as the morning light hit my sleepy eyes. Wiggling my toes, I looked around, slowly remembering where I was.

I rearranged some crazy morning bedhead and dragged myself downstairs to the kitchen. Rhys's pillow was still perched against the arm of the sofa where he slept the night before.

I wonder what he sleeps in. Is he a pajamas kind of guy?

"Breakfast will be done in five," Rhys said, nodding at

the corner. "Coffee's there."

It was only after my first gulp of coffee that I realized how weird this situation was.

"Have you ever done an assignment with a partner before?" I wrapped my hands around the coffee mug to warm my fingers.

"Yeah. I work with another girl—er, woman—occasionally but she didn't quite pass Audrey's high standards for this assignment." He flipped the bacon and it hissed in the pan. "Some jobs just require more than two hands. Like tonight's."

"Should be a fun one." *Mmmm. Caffeine.* "What do you know about these two paintings we're picking up?" I licked my upper lip, savoring every drop of the delicious brew.

"One's a portrait of the ex-wife and one's a portrait of their baby."

"They had a child together?"

"Well, kind of." Rhys smirked. "A terrier. It had to be put down around the time of the divorce. Probably made things even sadder than they were already."

"Who gets a portrait done of their dog?"

"Rich people." He put down a plate of bacon and toast.

"You didn't meet the ex-wife, did you?"

"Of course not. Audrey would never let one of us near a client." He sipped his coffee and sat down with a plate for himself. "Her name is Ivy Dixon. She's well-known on this side of the pond."

I thought for a moment. "Isn't she an actress or something?"

"She used to be a supermodel. Big celebrity, lots of high fashion stuff, lots of sexy lingerie. Best Bod in Britain, I believe they called her." Rhys chewed on some bacon. "Out of nowhere, she finds religion and becomes an advocate for modesty and traditional family values. She wrote a bestseller on being a good wife over having a career. She did a ton of publicity to promote it. She also bashed the fashion industry and specific people within it. It was around this time she married boring old Albert Chandler, our target."

Poor bastard. Well, poor rich *bastard.*

"Needless to say, it angered a lot of people, especially people in the fashion industry. But then they got to have the last laugh when she had an affair and she and her husband divorced two years later. That was a few months ago."

"And where is she now?"

"London, I believe. Despite the infidelity, she got a huge settlement from her ex. She's probably working on another book about the importance of a faithful marriage or something."

* * *

The best thing about breaking into an old manor like Chandler House is the lack of nosey neighbors. Vast gardens and grounds surrounded the red-bricked building on all sides. The closest house was about a mile away and the people who lived there didn't appear to be home. It was perfect.

It was past 11 p.m. Rhys and I sat in the dark under a tree on a hill overlooking the manor. Albert had long since departed for the train station and most of the staff had left. All but one.

"I fuckin' hate butlers." Rhys lowered his binoculars and shone his flashlight at me. "Hold on a second… Why are you still wearing that ring? I'll need that back, just so you know."

"Why do you need it back this very second?"

"You never know when the right woman is gonna come along."

My eyes narrowed. "You are not seriously going to re-use this specific ring to propose to someone. That is so tacky!"

"It's a nice ring!" He smirked. "I stole it from Madonna."

I crossed my arms over my chest. "No way. You're full of shit."

"Okay. I made that up. It's still nice and I would like to have it back. So just take it off your damn finger!"

"I can't get it off my finger," I snapped. "It's too small."

"Are you sure your fingers aren't just too fat?"

"Shut up." I adjusted my sitting position and wiped some blades of damp grass from my knees. My ass was going numb.

"This chap isn't a live-in butler and he doesn't stay here when Chandler is out," Rhys said, his face hidden behind binoculars. "I don't know what the hell he's doing."

I lifted my binoculars. "Looks like paperwork."

"For two hours?" He shook his head and rolled his eyes.

Or at least I assumed he rolled his eyes. We were sitting in the pitch-black night with only the stars and the thumbnail-shaped moon as company. Besides a few crickets and the whistling wind, it was quiet. I was relieved the rain had stopped.

Something moved in the branches above us. Dropping

my binoculars, I stared up.

Rhys propped himself up on his elbows, looking up the tree. "It's probably just a wildcat."

I looked at him. "A what?"

"Scottish wildcat. They're like small tigers."

My eyes widened. "That's a thing?"

"Yeah. They feast on the blood of Americans."

"You're an asshole."

"Calm down." He laughed quietly. "I think it's a squirrel." Rhys took out his smartphone. "Security system is still off." He typed something on the screen.

I glanced at him and picked up my binoculars again. "What are you doing?"

"Looking up porn."

"Now?"

"Joking." He smiled. "Speaking of which, are you some sort of deviant?"

I whipped my head to look at him. "No. Why do you ask?"

"Your browser history."

I raised my eyebrow. He shrugged.

"You occasionally read steamy erotica, that's all." He turned his phone so I could see the screen—and there it was. My browser history from my home computer. Everything. Books on Amazon I'd looked at recently, videos I'd watched on YouTube, things I'd searched on Google ... and other stuff.

My cheeks felt warm. I punched Rhys on his shoulder.

"Would you knock it off?" I hissed. "I take it you don't know the meaning of privacy."

"Not yours."

I could feel him grinning at me in the dark.

I could murder him right after we get the paintings. No one needs to know.

Rhys sat up. "I think he's leaving." He looked at his phone and I watched the butler type a four-digit security code into a panel located just inside the front door. I watched where his finger went as he pressed—bottom middle, top middle, top left and then the first button on the second row.

"The security code is zero, two, one, four."

Rhys nodded, still watching his phone. "How romantic."

I smiled. "Second month, fourteenth day. Valentine's Day."

"Probably the day he and the ex-wife had their first date or something." He looked up from his phone and showed me the screen. "Security system is on."

Hacking into a security system: there's an app for that.

Rhys clicked and typed on his phone while I watched the butler drive off. He'd left several lights on in the main part of the manor, and they cast a large circle of light around the building.

Per my usual routine, I waited a few minutes to make sure the butler wasn't coming back because he forgot something. This gave Rhys time to get into the alarm system and disable the security cameras located outside *and* inside the house.

The butler still hadn't come back after fifteen minutes.

I nodded at Rhys. "Go for it."

He typed and tapped a few more times. "Aaaand..." Tap, tap, tap, *beep*. "We're good."

I slid my fingers into a pair of thick gloves. We left our

spot under the tree, making sure to stay low to the ground, just in case a car drove by on the nearby road.

We headed for the back of the manor. As expected, the lights were off in those rooms.

"Ya know, lots of people read erotica," I whispered. "It's very normal."

Rhys snickered and pulled on his own gloves. "You just keep telling yourself that, sweet cheeks."

He pressed the key code into the panel by the door and it beeped and turned green. Easy, peasy. Mounted above the door at the back entrance was a security camera, pointed directly down at us. The light by the lens was dark instead of red or green—Rhys hadn't just paused the cameras, he'd killed them completely.

Nice.

We let ourselves into a long galley kitchen. Besides the sound of the tap dripping in the old basin sink, the house was deadly quiet.

I usually prefer to have *some* noise around when I'm on an assignment. Noise can cover any sounds I might make while I go about my business. But then again, noise also hides sounds I might want to hear while I'm, say, cracking a safe or something.

I followed Rhys up two wide staircases with polished wooden rails.

"Audrey said the paintings are in a locked storage room left of the small study on the third floor," Rhys said. "Hopefully he hasn't moved them since she moved out."

This house was enormous. If, by chance, the owner had moved the paintings, it would take hours to find them—or he could have moved them to a storage facility somewhere else. I didn't even want to think about that.

In spite of the long, dark hallway lit only by the windows at the very end, we found the room. Rhys leaned against the wall beside the door. I used a small flashlight to check out the door's lock. Like almost everything in the house, the lock was old. Newer, modern locks are usually a lot more complicated than antique ones. It took me about a minute to unlock it using a bobby pin and a narrow metal tool I invented myself. And by invented I mean I bought it at the grocery store. It was just hanging out with the nutcrackers but I knew it would be useful when I saw it—with or without walnuts involved.

I turned the knob and the door opened with a low creak. Success!

"Molly," Rhys whispered, "get in that room right now."

I looked up at him. His face was frozen and he was staring down the corridor. I looked over my shoulder and saw the shape of a large dog in the light at the end of the hall. Its eyes glowed and its snarls grew louder and deeper as it lunged toward us.

I almost peed my pants. For reals.

"Now, Molly!" Rhys whipped the door open and I slipped inside.

Rhys tried to close the door behind us but the edge of it hit the dog's head. It yelped, and it only made the dog's growls scarier and angrier. While I pulled on the door, Rhys pushed on the dog's snout with his foot. The dog twisted its head around and clamped down on the end of Rhys's boot.

"Son of a bitch!" he yelled.

He whipped a syringe out of his pocket, took the cap off with his teeth and jabbed it into the dog's neck. The angry canine's eyes slowly closed and Rhys's foot fell from its jaws. The dog's heaving shoulders slumped down and it fell to one side. Shoving the dog's snout out of the way, Rhys pushed the door closed. He slid his back against the door and sat on the floor, catching his breath.

He took off his gnarled boot and surveyed the damage. "Audrey's buying me new boots." There were two holes in his sock and only a few specks of blood around the tears. I didn't see any blood on the floor either.

In a best-case scenario, we'd get these paintings out and Albert Chandler would never know we were here. He might not realize the paintings had been stolen for weeks, even months. If, by chance, we left behind any evidence linking us to this room, the cleaning staff would most likely take care of it before anyone noticed the paintings were missing.

In a worst-case scenario, Rhys would lose a foot, die of blood loss and someone would find his dead body being used as a chew toy by that dog out in the hall. Actually, losing Rhys along the way wouldn't be *that* horrible...

I crossed my arms over my chest. "Audrey didn't say anything about the Hound of Baskervilles living here!"

Rhys glared at me. "That's an English reference, not Scottish."

"Arthur Conan Doyle was Scottish, wasn't he?"

Another glare. Apparently having a foot mauled by a terrifying dog makes some people lose their sense of humor.

"What did you just jab that dog with?" I said. "It's not dead, is it?"

"Unfortunately not!" he hissed. "A weak tranquilizer. That dog is huge. He'll likely wake up before we're even done here."

My shoulders fell. "Are you serious?"

He nodded and put his mangled boot back on. "I hope you can climb."

I looked around. The room was crammed with boxes. At least thirty paintings of various sizes were stacked up against the walls. Dust swirled in the low light that filtered in from the window. I wasn't a huge fan of the idea of climbing out that window with a painting under my arm, but it was better than being a snack for Cujo out in the hallway.

"Are you okay?" I looked down at Rhys's mangled boot.

"I'll live." He pointed to a line of paintings on the wall. "You start on this side, I'll take that side."

Using our flashlights we checked all the paintings in the room, trying not to move them too much from their original spots. The job would've gone a lot faster if we turned on the light, but we didn't dare. I found the portrait of the terrier first.

"Cute little thing," I said, shining my flashlight on it. She was white and fluffy, with big black eyes and a little pink ribbon around her neck, sitting on a pink silk cushion, looking as regal as a Westie can. The painting was small enough that I could fit it under my arm.

"Oh, dear. Look at this."

I looked over my shoulder. Rhys was holding up a large canvas. I aimed my flashlight at it. It was a painting of a nude woman, peering seductively over her shoulder with her full lips parted, her back to the artist.

I raised my eyebrows. "That's Ivy, right?"

"Yup."

"Is that the right painting?" I slid off my gloves and stuffed them into my pocket.

Rhys looked closer at the signature in the corner of the canvas. "It's gotta be. The date's from six months before the divorce. It was done *after* she got that book published. This would cause a scandal." He put the painting back down. "I don't think she ever really lost her wild side at all. She just wants to hide."

"And destroy the evidence."

He nodded and looked at the window. "How the hell are we gonna do this?"

There was movement from the other side of the door. Cujo was waking up.

"If we don't get out soon, that dog is going to tear up the floor out there—or just come through the door." Rhys stared at the portrait and eyed the window. "We can get it out of here if we go at an angle. Shouldn't be an issue. But we're gonna have to put a hole in the floor to drill a mount for the climbing gear. There's nothing in here to tie the rope to."

I stared at the window, thinking hard. "We can tie the rope around the portraits and lower them down. Then we'll climb down. I'd say it's about a thirty-foot climb, maybe forty. Easy."

"Okay." He winced.

I sighed. "What?"

"I don't … love climbing. But I'm fine. In fact, I'm very good at climbing. Hell, I'm an *ace* climber. I just *prefer* using the mount and climbing gear."

I grinned. "Are you scared of heights?"

"No." He laughed. "Of course not."

"Are you sure?"

He hesitated. "Yes?"

I rolled my eyes. "We don't have time. Let's just do this."

He scoffed as I gave him one of the large garbage bags I'd brought in my kit to wrap around the paintings and protect them in transit.

I tied the rope around the terrier painting, one loop around the long side and one loop around the short side— that way it wouldn't slide out and crash to the ground. I lowered it out the window and slid it down the roof shingles and off to the side. I kept a close eye on it to make sure it didn't bang into anything on the way down. I scanned the area around the manor, just in case any neighbors happened to be going for a midnight stroll, as I slowly released the rope from the window.

Rhys hooked his rope up with the portrait of Ivy the same way and slid it through the window at an angle. He pushed it off the side of the roof and held tight to the rope. He took a deep breath, exhaled slowly and gently released the rope. It swung in the wind but didn't hit anything on the way down.

Heavy, frantic sniffing, growling and digging sounds came from the door, growing louder and louder. There was definitely going to be damage to the floor from that dog's claws. So much for not leaving any signs of our presence.

Rhys quickened his pace and I put on a pair of climbing gloves. Once the bigger painting was safe on the ground, I hoisted myself out of the window and started the climb down the side of the building.

Keeping close to the wall, I reached for any bit of stone that I could grip. My heart pounded hard in my chest. I tried to avoid looking down. As soon as there was room under the window, Rhys climbed down after me.

I reached for the ledge of a window but didn't put much weight on it. My arms and legs ached and my fingers throbbed. I looked up to check on Rhys.

"Nice ass," I said.

"Thanks," he said. "Your tits look great from this angle."

I pressed my foot to a bit of brick jutting out and held onto the window ledge. I put a bit more weight on the brick and it crumbled beneath me in a cloud of dust.

"You alright?"

I held on to the window ledge for dear life as my feet scrambled to find another secure bit of rock.

"Yup. I'm fine."

Sweat rolled off my chin as I made my way down a foot lower. I took a few deep breaths, exhausted from holding myself up by my fingers.

"I'm gonna jump down."

"Okay. Just don't land on the paintings."

I rolled my eyes. A "Be safe!" would have been nice.

I slowly and carefully got myself turned around while holding on to a nearby gable. I've always been better at climbing than falling.

I should have taken gymnastics in school like Mom wanted. Dammit.

I pushed myself off from the wall and bent my legs. I came *this close* to landing on the Ivy painting and rolled two or three times. My forearms got a bit scratched up but it could've been worse.

Rhys climbed down slower than me, taking his time to secure his footing before making each move.

He really does have a nice bum.

"I don't mean to pressure you, but we gotta hit the road. Time's a-tickin.'" Frowning, I tapped my wrist.

"Have I mentioned that I don't care for heights?" Clinging to a ledge, he stared straight ahead, his body rigid.

"Yeah, I kinda figured. You're gonna have to jump, Rhys. It's only a few feet. You can do it."

"Bollocks," he said, glancing at me over his shoulder. "That's at least six meters."

"I don't know how long a meter is compared to a foot."

Rhys sighed and got himself turned around halfway so one hand was gripping a window ledge and one edge of his foot was on resting on a lower window frame. He jumped, his eyes squeezed shut. He landed safely with bent knees, one hand on the ground. He stood up and smiled, looking very pleased with himself.

We headed into the thicket behind Chandler House, each carrying a painting. From there, Rhys turned the security cameras back on and we began the slow, careful trudge past prickly shrubs and wet mossy undergrowth.

Rhys stumbled over loose grass and mud, nearly falling over. Because of the awkward size, he had to hold the painting of Ivy Dixon in front of himself like a shield.

It started pouring. I let out an exasperated groan, my

stringy, soaked hair sticking to my face with rain dropping into my eyes.

Rhys burst out laughing. "What are you so mad about?"

"Why do you even *choose* to live here?"

"It's a little rain. You'll survive."

"You could literally live anywhere in the world." I stopped for a break under a tree. "Paris. The Bahamas. You could live in Italy! Uh, you could live in … uh, Sweden!"

"Why would I live in Sweden?"

"I don't know! They have a strong economic climate!"

The rain poured down even harder. Each drop hit every leaf in the trees around us. I looked up into the trees, just in time for a bird to come diving out at my face, screeching and cawing. I screamed and dove out of the way, whipping the canvas in front of my face. Rhys laughed loudly and shook his head.

I frowned at him. "I hate Scotland."

* * *

The next morning Rhys and I drove to Edinburgh with the paintings stowed in the trunk. He was quiet so I just slept, leaning my head against the window. I only woke up when we parked outside of a deserted golf course.

I looked around. "This doesn't look like Edinburgh."

Rhys turned off the engine and leaned against the car, checking his phone. I got out and stretched. The air was foggy and gray. I pulled my sweater tighter.

A minute later a silver town car pulled up beside us. A man in a black suit and sunglasses got out and opened the passenger side door.

"Good day," Audrey said, adjusting her black, wide-brimmed Kentucky Derby style hat as she got out of the car.

Rhys opened the trunk without a word and started unwrapping the paintings. Audrey crossed her arms over her chest and watched from the side.

"These *are* the right paintings, I presume," Rhys said.

Audrey didn't even blink at the risqué painting of Ivy Dixon. "Yes, that's correct."

She nodded to her driver. He wrapped them back up loosely and moved them from his trunk to hers.

"I assume everything went as planned," she said.

"Yeah," I said. "I mean, there was a rabid dog in the house we didn't know about but other than that—"

"It was fine." Rhys threw a look at me.

Oh, sorry! Didn't realize the adults were talking.

"Wonderful. My client will be thrilled to hear it. I'll have your payment wired to you within the day." She went back to her car. "I'll be in touch."

Back on the road again, Rhys wove between cars on the highway as we made our way to the airport. The wipers squeaked as they waved back and forth across the windshield.

"I'm surprised Ivy Dixon doesn't have her own reality show by this point."

He smirked and kept his eyes on the road. "She's too hot for TV. Maybe in fifteen years, after she's butchered her face with plastic surgery."

"Do you know what Ivy will do with the painting of her once she gets it back? Would she have it destroyed or hang it up in her house?"

He glanced at me. "Does it matter?"

"If I looked like that, I would consider hanging that painting up."

"Let me know if you ever get a portrait done. I'll come by your place and check it out."

I laughed out loud and shook my head. "You are never seeing my apartment. Creep."

He grinned. "Never?"

"Never *ever.*"

We arrived at the airport. Instead of finding a parking space, Rhys stopped at the front entrance. I got my suitcase out of the back seat.

I leaned down and looked through the window. "Uh, I guess this is goodbye." I shrugged. *What the hell do I even say to this guy?*

"We'll see," he said. "Have a good flight." And then he sped away, the tires screeching.

My first flight was from Edinburgh to London. All this traveling was taking a toll on my body and brain. I could barely remember what day it was, let alone how long I'd been in the United Kingdom.

I waited at Heathrow for my flight back to New York. My eyelids felt heavy and I fought to keep my head upright in my seat.

Must not fall asleep. Some creep will take my bag. Must ... not ... fall...

My phone vibrated in my pocket and my eyelids flicked open. There were two emails waiting for me. The first was from Audrey, letting me know my money had transferred successfully. The second email was to my personal 'Molly

Miranda' account, sent to me from my Betty Bruce email account a minute before.

What the heck is this?

To: mollymiranda
From: bettybruce
Subject: no subject
Molly,

As soon as you get home, you will wire every penny of that $500,000 you just received from Audrey to the transit number in the attached document. You have one day to do this. If you don't cooperate, I will flag your name in the FBI database and make sure they know who you are and what crimes you have been involved with.

Have a lovely trip home. I'm sure we'll be in touch soon.

Your pal,

Rhys

That son of a bitch.

CHAPTER FIVE

"Molly?"

My head jerked up and I scanned the room.

Where the heck am I?

Ah. Right. The living room sofa. Of course.

Nate peered down at me, coffee cup in hand. His hair was messy and he had a good amount of stubble along his jawbone. God, he was pretty. I slid back down into the sofa cushions. "What?"

"Why are you sleeping out here?"

"I got home late."

"I know. I heard you." He smiled. Oh, that smile.

"Sorry about that." I pulled a blanket off the back of the couch and draped it over myself.

Nate sipped his coffee. "But why are you out here and not in your room?"

I peered up at him.

Because I decided I couldn't go to bed until I figured out what to do about Rhys and the fact that he's stealing half a million dollars from me. No big deal. Somewhere in there, I must've fallen asleep on the couch. What's the difference? Leave me alone!

I pulled the blanket up to my chin. "One of the neighbors was yelling. I could hear it through the wall."

"Oh, I didn't hear anything."

I closed my eyes again, exhaustion tugging at my whole body.

"How's your aunt?"

"What?"

"Aunt Grace?"

Ah, shit. Right. That ol' (made-up) dame.

"She's fine."

"Good, glad to hear it. I was worried because you didn't text me back."

"I didn't get a text," I mumbled. "I think something is wrong with my phone."

My eyes were still closed but I heard him place his coffee mug in the sink and walk down the hallway to the bathroom.

I must've fallen asleep again because I didn't see or talk to Nate the rest of the morning. I woke up again around eleven to a silent apartment. All I could hear was the rage-filled voice in my head.

How could I let this happen?

Could I have prevented a genius-level hacker from finding out my identity? Maybe. Maybe not. But there was one person who needed to know what was going on.

I rummaged through my suitcase and found my phone in the front pocket.

"Hello, Betty," Audrey said in her usual holier-than-thou voice. "I assume you're back in New York now."

"Have you heard anything from Rhys?" I wasn't in the mood for small talk.

"No. Should I have?"

"I just thought you might be interested to know that he knows my real name, where I live, who my parents are. Everything."

And the erotica I read!

"And he's threatened to hand me over to the FBI on a silver platter."

Audrey was silent for a moment. "In exchange for what?"

"Five hundred thousand dollars."

"Ah."

I waited for her to continue. She didn't. "So, that's it then?"

"Well," she said, "obviously I won't be hiring him again."

"You said he was legit!"

"Legit?"

"Trustworthy."

"He seemed to be."

"You mean there's *nothing* we can even do about it?"

"Well, you know that old saying: No honor amongst thieves."

My eyes narrowed. *Of course* she'd say something like that. It's not like that phrase hadn't been floating around my brain since I received that stupid email.

"Has this ever happened before?" I said through a clenched jaw.

"Oh, most certainly."

I rolled my eyes. *A little warning would have been nice.*

"Do we have any contact info for this guy?" I stared at

the ceiling. "I don't even know his last name. But whatever he told you, I'm sure it's fake. I don't even know if he's actually Scottish! He used, like, five different accents—"

"I'm sorry, Betty, I can't give you his contact information."

"Why not?"

"That's confidential."

"Bullshit." I paced the living room. "If you're not going to hire him again, what's the difference if you give out his information or not?"

"I have a reputation to uphold." I could tell from her tone she was getting annoyed with me, as usual. "This is a very tight-knit field. He'd tell someone I gave out his information and then you'd be my only ... employee."

I rolled my eyes again. *I'm not your employee, lady. I'm a contract burglar. It's not hard to say.*

"By the sounds of it, you likely don't want to trifle with this man. If he really could do as much damage as you say, then why tempt him?"

Because he's blackmailing me, that's why!

I dropped onto the sofa again. "Fine. I'm out half a mill but whatever!"

"There's a good girl."

I will not throw my phone at the wall. I will not throw my phone at the wall.

"Anything coming down the pipeline I should know about?"

"Probably not until later this month." She paused. "Betty, let me call Rhys. Maybe he'll change his mind about this threat business once he knows I won't hire him again."

I felt better for about half a second. It was the most

considerate thing Audrey had ever said to me—but she was likely more concerned about losing the services of a hardcore hacker like Rhys than seeing me lose out on some cash.

We hung up and I went to have a shower. My skin was saturated with the smells of airports and airline food. My hair was matted and tangled from wearing a crappy wig during my flight from London to New York.

When I got out of the shower, there was an email notification on my phone.

To: bettybruce
From: audreyfox
Subject: situation
He handed in his notice. Turns out he's been freelancing for months. Sorry for the inconvenience.

Inconvenience? She thinks this is an inconvenience? *Are you kidding me? It's half a million dollars, not a traffic detour!*

* * *

I strolled into a tiny pawnshop in Brooklyn, located between a dry cleaners and a diner, and nodded at the man behind the counter. Jewelry, collectables, dishes, books and watches filled the shelves and display cases lined the walls. An antique chest sat in the corner, a 'Not for Sale' sign taped to it. Not many people know about the bloodstain under that chest, but that's a story for another time.

The man crossed his arms over his chest, tilting his head, a twinkle in his eye. His tiny dark eyes were almost hidden completely under thick, graying eyebrows. The lines around his eyes deepened as his thin mouth spread into a smile.

"Look what the cat dragged in."

A stout woman with a pile of salt-and-pepper curls appeared from the back room, her necklaces clicking. She rushed over and threw her arms around me. Her bright head scarf scratched against my cheek.

"We haven't seen you in ages!" She stepped back and looked at me over the round glasses sitting low on her pointed nose. "You look thin. You should eat more."

The man frowned. "Deanne. Don't bother the young lady."

"Hello, Paul."

"Hello, Betty." He nodded at me, looking very serious. *He knows something is up.*

I didn't even have to ask. Deanne planted herself at the front counter so Paul and I could talk in the back room.

Paul, my former employer, owns the pawnshop but makes his meat-and-potatoes from the same job Audrey does—contracting thieves to acquire specific items. I think he probably has hit men in his employ as well but I've never asked.

I still see Paul occasionally since his pawnshop is close to Ruby's office. I sometimes pop in to say hi or for, ahem, "other" business.

Paul and Deanne McCoy are two of the sweetest, hardest-working people I know, especially within the business. Deanne knows how Paul makes most of his money and she's okay with it. Both of their sons have medical school paid for because of his line of work. She loves bragging about her sons becoming doctors. The ladies she plays cards with are very jealous.

Paul offered me a chair in his office and sat behind his messy desk. He rested his hands on a few scattered papers, folding his pudgy fingers together.

"What can I help you with, missy?"

I took an envelope out of my purse, set it on the desk and slid it closer to him. Paul opened it and nodded at the diamond ring inside.

"You should know I'm happily married already." He smiled.

"Aw, shucks. I was hoping to make an honest man of you after all these years."

Paul slid his glasses on and checked it over with his hand lens, holding it up to the light to check the sparkle and clarity. The enormous stone was mounted on a gold band.

"And where is this little bauble from?"

"I picked it up during an assignment in London last year and just held onto it."

That was a lie. I'd finally managed to get Rhys's ring off my finger earlier that morning by rubbing butter around my knuckle. If Rhys was content to blackmail me, then I would happily sell his ring.

Paul peered at me over the top of his glasses. "So why are you bringing it to me today?"

I scratched the back of my neck. "Audrey paired me up with a guy who proceeded to screw me out of a half a million dollars, so I could use the cash."

"I see." His eyes narrowed as he considered the ring's value. "I'll give you seven grand."

"Seven? Are you kidding?" I sat back in my chair. "It's

worth at least twelve."

"Not in this economy. Best I can do is nine. I can wire you some money tonight."

"Deal."

Paul sat back in his chair, folding his arms across his torso. "Who's this fella you worked with?"

"His name is Rhys … something." I winced, realizing that finding him might not be easy, or even possible. "He's Scottish. Good at hacking security systems. Happen to know him?"

"Doesn't ring any bells. Is he new?"

I shrugged. "I've never heard of this guy before but Audrey made it sound like he'd been around the block a bit, like I was the amateur between the two of us."

"I know you don't play well with others," Paul glanced at me, "but knowing someone who can hack into security systems could be a real asset to you."

"You did hear me say he screwed me out of half a mill, right?"

He rolled his eyes. "Yes, you worked real hard for that money, missy."

My shoulders dropped. He might have had a point.

* * *

A few streets away from Paul's pawnshop, there's a small but elegant office with glass doors. Etched on those doors is the logo for the Cedar & Watson accounting firm.

I flipped through an old issue of *Cosmo* in the waiting room while the receptionist behind the desk texted. She looked disgusted. But she always looks that way. It might just be how her face is.

Ruby Watson is probably one of the youngest people in New York to co-own a successful accounting firm. She worked at another firm for a few years, became friends with a co-worker and they started the company together. She likely could have used a few more years of experience but hated being told what to do by her ten different bosses, all men over fifty and all fans of words like "synergy."

Eli Cedar came out of his office with a folder and smiled at me.

"Oh, uh, hi Molly." He gave a little awkward wave. "Ruby should be with you shortly." He glanced at the receptionist. "Tara, did you offer Molly a coffee?"

Tara barely looked up from her phone. "No."

I smiled weakly at Eli. "I'm fine."

"Are you sure? I can get you a water or … or—"

I don't know if Ruby realizes it, but the girl knows how to make an entrance.

Eli's face flushed as Ruby stepped out of her office. A braided leather headband kept her piles of golden brown curls in place. A white lace dress hugged her hourglass frame and brown lace-up boots made her long legs look even longer. She tossed a folder onto the front desk.

How Ruby and Eli even became friends, I have no idea. Well, okay, maybe I have *some* idea. Eli fell in love with her instantly and is now stuck in the friend zone. Meanwhile, Ruby will pretty much befriend anyone but knew she needed someone a bit older, with more experience, if she wanted to have her own business. And now she does.

"Hey girl," Ruby said, her voice as soft as honey. "Come on in."

Eli immediately stared at his shoes and fled back into his office. Poor Eli. I wonder if he's met any of Ruby's boyfriends. Her occasional boyfriends are always super attractive, have amazing bodies, perfect hair and usually treat her like a goddess. But it never lasts. Ruby bats for both teams and usually prefers women. She says they smell nicer.

I slunk into Ruby's office and rested my forehead against the window. I could see right into the office across the street but Ruby assured me it's the most boring office ever. Twenty or so stories up and just a layer of glass between me and the outside world.

If heights scared me, I'd be in another profession.

"The poo has hit the fan, my friend."

"What poo is this?" Ruby flopped down on the brown leather sofa she keeps in her office for when she needs a nap.

That's what kind of office she keeps. And I think that's awesome.

"I went to Aberdeen a few days ago." I glanced at her. "That's in Scotland."

"I knew that."

I raised my eyebrow at her.

"I did not know that." She shrugged.

"I worked with a guy on this assignment, and after it was finished and I was on my way back home, he contacted me again. He's going to hand me over to the FBI if I don't give him my share of the payment from this job."

"And how much is that?"

"Five hundred thousand."

"Ouch." She frowned. "Do you happen to have his bank information? I might be able to track down some info on him for you, if you need me to."

"Yes! That would be fantastic! I'll forward you the transit number I have."

Ruby crossed her arms over her chest and nodded. "I thought you didn't work with partners."

"I don't! But Audrey insisted. Honestly, this job would likely have been difficult with just one person. I just wish Audrey hadn't paired me with a blackmailing scumbag."

Ruby is one of the few people who know what I do for a living. Back when I was still working for Paul, he recommended I go see her since I was starting to have too much unaccounted-for cash in my bank account. He sent me to Ruby because she has no qualms about doing business with people like me—professional criminals. She knows how to hide suspicious transactions and spread money efficiently between several accounts to avoid the ever-watchful eye of The Man.

I guess, technically, that makes Ruby a professional criminal too. But she gets to do it with a fancy office and her name on the door. No air travel required.

"Have you sent the five hundred thousand to him?"

"Not yet. I was hoping to come up with a plan, but nothing yet. Audrey can't even do anything about it." I sat on the end of the sofa. "Does Eli have any idea what I do?"

She shook her head. "I told him your parents own a ski lodge. That's the story I'm supposed to go with, right?"

I nodded. "I even told Nate that lie." I frowned.

"I'm horrible."

Ruby lifted her head off the sofa. "Oh my *god.*"

"What?"

"You slept with him."

I stared at her. "Wha-what?"

"You and Nate finally had sex." She threw her arms up in the air. "Hallelujah!"

I felt my cheeks becoming warmer. "Are you always so concerned with the sex your *cousin* may or may not be having?"

She shrugged. "I don't really care about his sex life as much as I care about *your* sex life. How was it?"

I searched for the right words, my mouth twisted. "It was … nice."

Ruby sighed loudly and let her head fall back onto the arm of the sofa. "How disappointing."

"You're gross."

She shrugged again. "Perhaps." She sat up. "Well, do you *like* him?"

I hesitated. "Yeah."

Ruby burst out laughing. "Oh, honey. I was only joking. Everyone knows you're in love with that guy." And she kept laughing.

I glared at her.

"This is a good thing! Why don't you see where it goes?" She frowned at me. "And cheer the hell up. It's just a relationship, not a death sentence."

"Is it a real relationship if I have to lie to him about almost everything?"

"No, I think that's just marriage."

* * *

I stirred the vegetables and the sauce in the pan and double-checked the recipe on my phone.

Hopefully I won't be serving semi-frozen vegetables for dinner. Hell, I should've just ordered pizza. Better yet, I could have just hired an in-house chef for the evening. Ooh! Can I just have a chef come over to make all *my meals? "Yes, Pierre. Can you chef me up a stack of pancakes?" "Certainly, madame."*

Nate poked his head into the kitchen, looking genuinely alarmed. "Are you cooking?"

"Yes."

He paused. "Why?"

"Because that's what people do, I'm told." I eyed the sizzling pan. "And you made us breakfast the other day so I figured I'd return the favor and make us dinner."

Nate checked it out, giving it a quick stir with the wooden spoon. He smelled it cautiously and nodded in approval.

"How was work?" I asked.

"One of the waitresses spilled clam chowder on a customer," he said, grabbing a beer from the fridge for me and one for himself. "The guy was furious and started yelling at *me* for some reason. I wasn't even his waiter." He rolled his eyes.

Good god, waiting tables sounded miserable. On the other hand, most jobs sound miserable.

He smiled. "How was your day?"

My heart did that stupid flip-flop thing.

"Good." I busied myself with stirring, to avoid eye contact.

Nate turned on the TV. The evening news was doing a feature on a British charity that was pairing with an

American charity to do ... I don't know. Something. I wasn't paying attention. A familiar voice came from the television. I whipped my head around the corner.

Audrey Fox was standing behind a podium, smiling wide. *I've never seen her smile before.*

"What the shit?" I whispered.

Nate looked over his shoulder. "What?"

My eyes were glued to the screen. She was standing in front of a huge banner for a charity called The Fox-Hartford Foundation for Women. If she hadn't been speaking and wearing a Chanel suit, I might have thought it was just a lookalike, but there she was. Not hiding, not trying to blend in.

"We're so happy we could work together for such an important cause," she said before the audience clapped.

Audrey hiding in plain sight. It was kind of brilliant.

"Do you know her?"

I blinked at him. "No. Sorry. I thought it was someone else." I nodded. "Cate Blanchett. That's who she looks like."

After a mediocre stir-fry supper, we hung out on the sofa and chatted for a bit. Nate put his iPhone on the coffee table, turned on a slow indie rock ballad, stood up and held out his hand.

"What?" I smiled up at him. "Do you want a high five?"

"No, I'm trying to be romantic."

"The meal wasn't even that good. You don't have to—"

"But I want to."

I let out a nervous breath and took his hand. He pulled me in close, his hand on my lower back. His nose and soft lips brushed my forehead. Visions of the other night kept popping into my head like distant memories I'd tried to forget. A mixture of happiness, excitement and fear rose up from my stomach.

It wouldn't surprise me if he heard my heart pounding.

He tipped my chin up with his hand and kissed me lightly. His eyelashes tickled my skin. I looked up at him through my bangs and touched the front of his plaid shirt. He planted his hands on my hips and kissed me again, this time a bit harder and more determined. It felt so nice and effortless, like we'd kissed a thousand times before.

This time we ended up in my bedroom. I pushed my mangled blankets and my suitcase onto the floor. We made out for quite a while, our legs entwined. One after another, articles of clothing were peeled away.

This time around, it didn't feel like a frantic, now-or-never race. My heart somehow managed to push away my thoughts of fear and doubt.

But it couldn't push away my stubborn bladder.

I pulled my lips from Nate's. "I'm so sorry. I have to pee."

I slipped into the bathroom quickly and did my business as fast as I could. I tapped my bare toes on the linoleum as I went. I fluffed my hair a bit and reapplied my lip gloss in the mirror. I skipped back down the hall and leaned against my bedroom doorframe, trying to be sexy.

But Nate wasn't even looking at me. He was looking at something in his hand.

My passport.

"Who's Betty Bruce?"

CHAPTER SIX

If there is a lesson to be learned from any of this, it's this one: unpack your goddamn suitcase as soon as possible. And don't just push an open suitcase off your bed. Because it can ruin the mood big time.

It also has the potential to ruin your life.

I stared at Nate, my stomach turning. "What?" I said dumbly.

I was still wearing a bra and underwear but I've never felt so exposed in my life.

He didn't come any closer. We just stood at opposite ends of the room, looking at each other.

"Who is Betty Bruce? She looks exactly like you." He held it up so I could see the (hideous) photo in the front cover. "Is Betty your real name?"

Finally! Something I didn't have to lie about.

"No. My real name is Molly Miranda."

"Then tell me, who is this person?" He skimmed over

the pages with his thumb. "This thing's full of stamps. Do you have a twin who travels a lot or something?"

Just say yes.

"No." I swallowed and exhaled slowly. "I don't have a twin."

He flipped to the last page that was stamped. "The last stamps in here are from yesterday and Saturday." He looked back at me, his eyes full of confusion and anger. The puzzle pieces were coming together in his head. "You didn't go to Vermont, did you?"

I felt sick. I opened my mouth to speak. Nothing came out. What could I possibly say?

"Do you even have an Aunt Grace?"

I looked at my feet. I was back to not being able to make eye contact.

It wasn't like I'd never lied to people before but lying to Nate felt ... different.

"Molly, would you just talk to me?" He looked at the most recent page of my passport again. "Heathrow? You were in Britain for three days?" He looked at a few other pages.

I winced. "Could you keep your voice down?"

He only got louder. "Why? Why do I have to keep my voice down? What's going on?"

"I was there for work." I clenched my jaw and snatched the passport from his hand. "Just chill the fuck out, alright?"

Nate glared at me and grabbed his jeans from the floor. "Is that all I get?"

I pulled my T-shirt back on and glared right back at him. "There are things about me I can't tell you. Why did you even look at this? *This* is none of your business."

"I like you, Molly, but I feel like I know nothing about

you. I don't even know your real name!"

"It's Molly," I snapped. "I just said that."

"Then who the fuck is Betty?"

Just say you have multiple personality disorder. There's at least a ten percent chance he will believe that.

"It's me ... as well." I shook my head and crossed my arms over my chest.

"But you can't explain why you have two names."

I hesitated. "Right."

Nate found his shirt and stormed out of my room. I heard the front door shut a minute later, a little more forcefully than I'd have liked.

I sat on the edge of my bed—formerly known as Molly's Bed of Love—and threw my passport against the wall, an action much more dramatic with something bigger and harder than a booklet.

My options were few, and none of them were ideal.

1. Tell him the truth and risk him hating me.

2. Tell him the truth and risk him hating me *and* going to the police.

3. Make up an elaborate, twisted lie with far too many strange details. This will at least make me look like something better than a thief and he can continue to adore me without guilt.

4. Take a flight to Florida, take on a new life and identity there and leave Nate and New York behind completely. I could find a different line of work, something less complicated. Maybe I could get a job playing a Disney princess at Disney World—it would be the perfect cover for someone like me. Maybe Cinderella.

My phone buzzed. I grabbed it, hoping it might be a text from Nate.

The number was a string of zeros. I rolled my eyes. There was only one person the text could be from: Rhys.

00000000000: *Hey sunshine. Still haven't seen that money yet. You've got an hour. Please don't consider not sending it to me. Ciao.*

I glared at the screen. I would not have been surprised if it cracked from the pressure. I didn't want to deal with Rhys right now but I knew I probably didn't have a choice.

I wasn't even sure if a text to a fake number would get to him, but I responded anyway.

Molly: *How do I know you won't fuck me over, even if I do send it to you?*

A few seconds later, this flashed onto my screen.

00000000000: *I guess that's just a chance you'll have to take.*

I threw my phone onto the bed and stared at the wall. My throat tightened and my vision blurred as tears formed in my eyes.

I have to do it. I have to send Rhys that money.

I felt utterly and entirely defeated.

If I told Nate the truth, there was a chance he himself would go to the police anyway. But if I didn't send Rhys the money, then he most certainly would do something to put my life in jeopardy, and I wasn't going to allow that to happen.

But if I don't send him the money and the FBI finds out who I am, I have the option of making a deal with them if I give them information on Rhys.

I shook my head as soon as the thought appeared. I didn't actually *have* any information on Rhys. That probably wasn't even his real name anyway. I had nothing on him and nothing to offer the FBI.

Besides, a British super-hacker is more of a CIA thing. Or would it be Homeland Security? I'm not even sure what the difference is.

That reminds me—I haven't watched the new season of Homeland *yet.*

In hindsight, finishing college and getting a real job probably would have been a good move, and I could've avoided this whole mess.

Yeah, right. Everyone coming out of college is finding a job right away. Hilarious!

I went to my computer and logged into my bank account. (Isn't online banking the best?) I stared at the screen, my finger hovering over the mouse button.

Hold on. There's still time to figure something out. He's just bluffing. But if I do send it, it's certainly not the end of the world. I have more money in the bank. I'll be fine, just as long as Audrey comes through with another assignment soon. Or I can get in touch with Paul. I'm sure he can set me up with something in the US.

I squeezed my eyes shut and clicked. My whole body tensed up as I read the confirmation screen. In a single click, my bank account was drained of five hundred thousand dollars. Seconds later, my phone buzzed again.

00000000000: *Good girl.*

CHAPTER SEVEN

"Now, if you're looking for something beautiful and fast, we've got the Mustang Convertible out there." The guy at the car rental place pointed to the red car in the lot closest to the window. "She's my favorite."

I gazed at it. She was certainly a pretty vehicle. I'm not the type of person who drools over cars. But the Mustang Convertible is not just a car and not just a way to get from point A to point B. This car made a statement. And that statement was "I'm fierce."

No need to waste money on a rental car that will stick out like a sore thumb. I need something to help me blend in.

Beside it was a blue Toyota.

"I'll take the blue one," I mumbled.

It was the day after Nate had stormed out. I was also five hundred thousand dollars poorer, thanks to Rhys. Things weren't going well.

Once I got a coffee and was out of the city, I sped down

the I-95. I'd made this journey a few times before.

If I tell Nate the truth and he decides to turn me in, what then? Do I make a run for it? Do I go to prison, serve my time and become a useful member of society? I wonder how much time I would serve. Probably a lot. Although wouldn't they need proof? And then there's the whole thing with Rhys. He may not even know as much as he thinks he does. Or he could know everything—

A nearby car blared its horn. I swerved a bit to the right so I wasn't, like, in the middle of the highway.

Maybe I should be focusing on the road and not the many ways my life is fucked right now.

I stopped for the night in a crummy motel in South Carolina. The sketchy white trash desk attendant hitched up her bra strap as she gave me the once-over.

"Are you travelin' alone?"

"Yes."

"Okay. That'll be a hundred and sixty-three dollars. How will you be paying today?"

You're kidding me. This shithole is a hundred and sixty-three dollars?

The room itself was just as bad as I thought. The air conditioner clunked and blew lukewarm air into the muggy room. The mini fridge was moldy inside and the TV looked like it was from the early nineties. And there were several suspicious-looking curly black hairs in the tub.

Fucking gross.

I woke up in the middle of the night to the sound of giggling from the next room, followed by a loud, creaking bed. Someone named Pearl was very impressed with someone named Billy Bob and was very vocal about his performance. I folded the pillow around my head to cover my ears. It didn't do much.

I banged on the wall. "Keep it down over there, I'm trying to sleep in here!"

"I'm sorry, little darlin.' You care to join us?"

They cackled to themselves and continued, even louder than before.

Exhausted, I left before seven the next morning. I got a coffee and drank it in the parking lot of the coffee shop, leaning against the hood of my car. The small town was pretty lame but at least it offered fresh air. A cop, his hand on his hip, strutted over to me.

Some people in my line of work don't like police officers, for obvious reasons. They are the enemy. But I have no problem with them—they're just doing their job. Just like I try to do mine.

"Mornin,' ma'am," he said with a nod, a coffee in his own hand.

I shuddered. *Ma'am.* Ew.

I nodded back and squinted into the early morning sun. "Good morning."

"I noticed you've got New York plates. What brings you to this part of the country?" He slurped his coffee loudly.

"I'm heading to Florida," I said. "Gonna have a little fun in the sun."

"That's great. I took the kids to Universal Studios last month, they loved it." He looked back at me. "You look familiar."

I felt my heart jump in my chest but I tried to keep a friendly, chilled expression. "Oh?"

"Yeah. I can't put my finger on it..." He shifted his weight and stared at me for a few seconds. "Are you an actress or something?"

I let out a startled laugh. "An actress? God, no." I shrugged. "I'm ... I'm nobody."

"Well, I'm sure you're not nobody. *No one* is nobody. Everyone is *some*body."

I smiled. "Poetic."

The police officer laughed and tossed his cup into a nearby garbage can. "You have a safe trip, ma'am." He nodded and got back in his car.

I got back behind the wheel, a little more awake now, and blasted the air conditioning. It was warming up fast outside.

This would certainly feel nicer in a convertible.

* * *

I received a text when I stopped for gas early that afternoon.

Ruby: *I'm bored. Where are you right now?*

Molly: *Key Largo.*

Ruby: *Is that the new place in SoHo? Seems a little chic for you.*

I rolled my eyes. *Thanks, Ruby.*

Molly: *No. Key Largo, as in Florida.*

Ruby: *SPRING BREAK WHOOOO!!!! (??)*

Molly: *I'll explain later. See you in a few days.*

Ruby: *TTYL. Love you.*

I put on some Jack Johnson, slipped on my giant sunglasses and drove, bright blue water on either side of me. I rolled down my window and let the salty sea air lick my cheek. Despite the troubles of the past few days, the ocean waves and the palm trees were already helping ease my anxiety.

Driving through Florida and into the Keys always makes me feel like I'm driving off the side of the country. Every available patch of earth is in use—docks, big homes, hotels and resorts. The only areas not packed in tight are the swampy bits lining the highway.

I turned down a narrow street lined with white sand and drove by the familiar houses, all painted fun, tropical oranges and blues. At the end of the street, I pulled into the driveway of a bright yellow house with white trim. White curtains fluttered in front of open windows on the second floor and onto a balcony. The tops of palm trees peeked out from behind the house and there was an orange tree in the garden. A sporty, silver two-seater convertible sat in the driveway next to a shiny black SUV.

I shook my head and smiled. *Why live in New York when I could have this?*

I slowly stepped onto the veranda and rang the doorbell, peering in the nearby window. I heard someone check the peephole before opening the door.

"Oh, my god," a voice said from the other side of the door and whipped it open.

A handsome older man wearing a terrible Hawaiian shirt stared at me and broke into a smile.

"Well," he said, a stunned look on his face. "Hello there!"

"Hi, Dad."

CHAPTER EIGHT

Dad, looking a bit grayer around the temples than I remembered, let me in.

"How the hell are you?" he said, pulling me in for a tight hug. "It's been a while! You should come down here more often, punkin."

I was a grown woman and he was still calling me 'punkin.'

"Same ol' story." I shrugged. "Life, busy, work. Et cetera."

He waved me inside and I flopped down onto his leather sofa. It felt nice and cool against my bare legs.

Dad sat next to me, stretching his arm across the back of the couch, like he always does. It was strange seeing him with such a golden-brown tan. When I was a kid, he was so fair he was basically translucent, like me.

He must've noticed me looking at his baked legs.

"You should put some sunscreen on. You're gonna burn to a crisp."

"I have some in my suitcase," I said. "Are you going to be

home for a few days? I could use a break. I probably should have called first. I've just been dealing with some stuff and—"

"Don't be silly. You're always welcome here." He sat back. "And I'm not going anywhere. You know I'm retired."

I nodded hesitantly. I couldn't tell if he was lying or not.

Dad didn't intentionally pass on the family business to me. It just kind of happened.

"Well, except for teaching karate on Wednesday evenings at the local YMCA." Dad smiled proudly, even though he pronounced it like *kah-rah-tay*. "Are you still kickboxing?"

"I switched to an aikido self-defense class." I frowned. "I only go occasionally, though. I think the sensei hates me."

I dabbed at my neck. Sweat. The Florida humidity was already showing up on my skin.

"You seem so at home here," I said. "It's so ... colorful."

He laughed. "I used to be like you. I used to think New York was the center of the universe. I've been a lot of places and this is the place for me."

"But ... alligators."

Dad shrugged. "We've got alligators, New York has drug dealers. And murderers. And prostitution. And—" He shuddered. "—Donald Trump."

"I don't know how much longer I'll be living there. Something's come up that could potentially—"

I heard movement upstairs and glanced at Dad. He shifted in his seat and an expression of pure discomfort and guilt washed across his face.

He has a girlfriend. And I've walked in on ... something. Well, that's awkward.

Dad paused. "That's ... a friend of mine. I should go tell

her we have company."

Before he could take two steps away from the sofa, a fair-skinned creature with long blonde hair and legs for days pranced down the wooden spiral staircase at the end of the room. She was wearing a wide sunhat, a semi-transparent beach cover-up dress and a tiny bikini. The brim of her sunhat and her dark sunglasses hid her face.

"Who was at the door?" she asked in a familiar English accent.

"*Audrey*?" I stared at her, glanced at my father and then back to her, adding everything up in my head.

My father is sleeping with Audrey Fox. How in the... No, I don't want to think about it. Ugh. And also ewwwwww.

Wide-eyed, she glared at me and frantically crossed her arms over her chest. I wasn't sure if it was because her bikini was revealing or if she was annoyed to see me.

I raised my hand in a little wave.

Audrey avoided eye contact and stayed standing on the staircase. "Didn't expect to see you here."

Dad sat back down. "Audrey, I believe you and Molly know one another."

I froze. She knew me as Betty.

"Oh, unclench, will you?" Audrey sat in the wicker chair across from the sofa, her arms still crossed. "I already know your real name is Molly." She rolled her eyes and pursed her lips in disgust.

Dammit, Rhys.

I had indeed interrupted something, probably a trip to the beach. I can't imagine Audrey's skin doing too well in this sun; she's fairer than I am. She already had a light tan, though, so she must've been with Dad for a while.

I looked at Dad and back at Audrey.

"Audrey and I are ... old friends?" He ended with an upward inflection.

"What your father is trying to say is that we occasionally visit one another for companionship." Audrey looked at me with cold, dead eyes. "Drinks, social events, shagging. That sort of thing."

Dad threw her a look.

I just stared at her. "Yeah, I got that from what *he* said. But thanks for clarifying."

She is intentionally trying to make me uncomfortable. Friends with benefits. Good god. Isn't fifty-something a bit old to have one of those?

"How did you guys even meet?" I said.

I knew Dad was an old acquaintance of Paul but I had no idea Audrey and Dad knew one another.

"It's a small world," Audrey said. "We know a lot of the same people."

Small world, all right. Far too small for my taste.

"Is it ... like ... serious between you two?" I hated to even ask.

Audrey scoffed. "Don't worry. I'm not going to be your new mummy, if that's what you're thinking."

Oh god. I hadn't even thought of that. As if two criminals in the Miranda family wasn't enough. A third would just make for a bad sitcom.

Dad, who looked about ready to climb inside the sofa to hide from this conversation, turned back to me. "*Anyway.* You should get out of New York. Too many people, not enough sunshine."

"But I've got the apartment now. And a roommate. And a ... problem."

I glanced at Audrey. She was staring intently at her perfect manicure.

I filled Dad in on the assignment with Rhys and the blackmail.

Dad's face stiffened. "How much does he want?"

"Five hundred thousand." I shrugged. "It's done. I sent it to him."

He crossed his arms over his chest. "I wish you would have called me first."

"I'm okay without the money for a little while, as long as someone comes through with some work for me very soon." I glanced at Audrey. She continued to avoid meeting my eyes.

"You should have called me first," Dad repeated.

"What, so you could've put a hit out on him? I know nothing about this person and Audrey wouldn't give me any information on him so I could track him down."

Her eye twitched as she continued to glare at me. Dad turned to her and waited for her to explain. She uncrossed her arms and folded her hands in her lap.

"In order to keep his contact information private and away from you, Rhys also dug up information about me. If I tell you anything about him, I might as well hand myself over to the authorities right now."

"Why did you hire this little prick in the first place?" Dad said, staring hard at Audrey. Frown lines appeared at the corners of his mouth as he clenched his jaw.

"How was I supposed to know he would go rogue so suddenly?" she blurted out. "He'd been a great employee until then and his record was clean."

I almost laughed when she said "go rogue." *Somebody's been watching too many spy movies.*

He looked back at me. "Do you need money?"

"No, I'm fine."

"That's another thing." She finally made eye contact with me. "Rhys wants me to hire someone else—someone of his choosing—for all upcoming assignments. He sees you as a threat. I'm not exactly in a position to say no."

"What you're saying is ... I've been replaced."

"You must know that I have no choice." She paused. "It's unfortunate but there's no other way."

We all have to do what we need to do to survive, I suppose.

I sat back and stared out the window, watching the curtains billowing. "Fantastic."

"You're a smart girl. I'm sure you'll land on your feet." Audrey cleared her throat. "Now, which hotel are you staying at while you're here?"

She barely had the words out of her mouth when Dad said, "She's staying here."

He was obviously not terribly impressed with Audrey, given that she'd screwed over his daughter and hadn't told him about it.

"Perhaps I'll leave then," she said.

Dad sighed. "Oh, come on—"

"No, no. That's fine." She was already up, heading back upstairs. "We wouldn't want the house to get too crowded. I've got to meet someone in Miami tomorrow morning anyway."

I smiled coolly. "Something related to your charity?"

Audrey adjusted the brim of her hat. "That is none of your concern but since you brought it up, how do you know about my charity?"

"It was on the news."

Dad raised an eyebrow. "You watch the news?"

"Yes," I snapped. "I'm an adult. I'm a very worldly person."

Audrey folded her slender arms in front of her and smiled smugly. "Where is Burkina Faso?"

France?

"Ladies, play nice." Dad shook his head at Audrey.

She ignored him and continued up the stairs.

Dad looked at me and rolled his eyes. "Women."

While she packed and prepared to leave, Dad made himself busy by pouring us orange juice. I'm not talkin' the stuff you get out of a carton, but with actual oranges. My father, who used to live on burgers and Starbucks, had gone organic since moving to Florida.

It was kind of bizarre.

"So," I said, "how long have you known I've been working for Audrey?"

My father and I have a long-standing agreement: he'll stay out of my professional life if I stay out of his. Only seeing one another occasionally makes the agreement easy to keep.

"I was one of your references for the job." He smiled weakly.

"And here I thought she hired me because I earned it."

"Oh, you have. But she trusts my judgment." He finished off his glass of juice. "I'm sure Paul could get you some work."

"I don't want to work so close to where I live. It doesn't feel safe."

Dad nodded. He, of all people, knows how precious security can be for a person in my career field. Once upon a time it was his career field, too. I had a feeling it still was.

"Ever think about ... leaving the business?"

"And do what?" I sipped my orange juice. "Jobs aren't exactly easy to find right now."

"I told you to finish university," he snapped.

"I know people who have master's degrees who are flipping burgers—"

"I'm leaving." Audrey stood by the door with a tiny black suitcase. She had changed from swimwear to a black dress—one could only assume Chanel. "Dean, I'm sure we'll be talking at some point."

Dad said goodbye to her at the door. They talked quietly just outside, kissed and she left, taking the black SUV with her.

Dad came back in. "I meant to ask about your mom. How is she?"

"Fine, I guess."

He grinned. "And Joe the plumber?"

"Joe is great. He's nice and he's good to Mom. He's ... present."

Dad winced. Between his various job assignments and a couple stints in prison, he'd been away a lot. Mom got lonely. Before the divorce proceedings were final, she and Joe were already very much in love. Dad was obviously still feeling the sting.

"What about your sister?"

I shrugged. "I honestly don't know. We don't talk."

"The two of you never really got along. I thought you might grow out of it."

"As far as I know, Haylee is enjoying a normal university experience."

Dad smiled. "Hopefully *she'll* actually finish."

As if one parent telling me I should have finished college wasn't enough.

"Did you say you have a roommate?"

"Yeah. I got tired of living by myself. He's great but…" I looked at the floor. "He … found my Betty Bruce passport."

"Oh." He nodded. "You could just threaten to evict him if he says anything about it. I'm sure his rent is more than reasonable."

"I'm not going to evict *or* threaten Nate. He's a friend." *And I love him.*

"Your mother still doesn't know you own the apartment, huh?"

I shook my head. He chuckled.

"What?"

"I was barely around when you were growing up," he said. "Yet I'm the parent who knows more about you."

I could never, ever tell Mom that I'd chosen a life of crime like Dad. It would break her heart. I couldn't do that to her.

"Does this Nate fellow know what you do?"

"No. I left New York before we could have that little chat. I don't know if I should tell him the truth or not—"

"Why the hell would you tell him the truth?"

"Because I don't like lying to people I lo—live with."

Dad took our glasses back to the kitchen and rinsed

them in the sink. "I'm not exactly the best person to ask for advice there, punkin."

No, Dad, you really aren't.

* * *

We ordered Chinese for supper and ate it on his boat tied up at the marina at the end of his street. It was nice to catch up.

Dad took a bite of an egg roll. "Sell the apartment."

I shook my head. "I'd really rather not."

"Oh, come on. Sell it and move here. You can stay with me as long as you like or buy a house for the same as what you paid for that cupboard you call a home. You could start a new life, a new career. Or..." He lowered his voice. "...there is plenty of work for you here."

I'm so lucky to have such an encouraging father—encouraging me to steal and whatnot.

As I sat on the boat, the sun dipping below the edge of the world, it was a tempting idea. A new life in sunny Florida. I could swim in the ocean any time I wanted.

Or get eaten by an alligator.

"I have a good thing going in New York," I said. "I can make it work."

My phone buzzed, notifying me of a new text message.

Nate: *Should I be worried?*

Molly: *No. I'm just visiting my dad out of state.*

Nate: *We should probably talk when you get back.*

At least it doesn't sound like he hates my guts ... as of this moment, anyway.

"Let me help you out financially."

I shook my head. "I'm not going to take your money."

"Alright." He nodded thoughtfully. "Then would you care to take someone else's money while you're here?"

"Seriously?"

"Why not?" He shrugged. "And don't even try to tell me you don't have your gear in the trunk of that car."

Damn. He had me there.

CHAPTER NINE

We drove to Key West the next evening. The sky turned overcast but the ocean breeze felt wonderful as we cruised along the sea-lined highway. The drive from Key Largo to Key West seemed to take forever as Dad and I ran out of things to talk about pretty quickly.

"Seeing anyone?"

"Nope."

He was silent for a few minutes.

"What about your roommate?"

"There's nothing going on there, okay? I thought there might be something but I went and fucked that up. So, just, never mind him."

Dad stared ahead at the stretch of highway before us. "I was just going to ask if he may cause you trouble … but I guess I don't know the whole story."

Dammit.

"Do you want to talk about it?"

"No." I stared out the window. "You should have let me drive."

"But you don't know where we're going."

"I *would* know if you'd just *tell* me."

"What's the fun in that?"

"I obviously take my job a lot more seriously than you," I snapped.

We eventually arrived in Key West and drove along a narrow street, encircling an aboveground cemetery.

"This is Key West City Cemetery," Dad said.

It was a creepy spot—a plot of land littered with white and blue-gray tombs, many of them stained with age and water spots. They appeared scattered randomly, some flat like slabs and others like miniature apartment buildings. Several were decorated much more lavishly than the plain ones right next to them. A black wrought iron fence surrounded the area. Homes bordered the cemetery, some right next to the fence—far too close for comfort. The setting sun vanished beneath the horizon, casting eerie shadows between the graves.

"Grave-robbing? You can't be serious."

Dad parked the car in the driveway of a small bungalow next to the fence. We watched as the shadows from the graves grew long and the sky slowly turned black.

"What if the people in the house see our car?" I whispered as we closed the car doors.

He shook his head. "They're friends of a friend and away six months of the year. Don't worry about it, punkin."

I followed him to a tree in the back yard. Dad hopped from one low branch to the higher ones. He seemed way more limber than most fifty-somethings. He reached for a lower branch.

"We're hopping the fence?" I whispered. "That's so juvenile."

"The lock on the front gate is huge." He grabbed another sturdy limb and hoisted himself up. "This is faster."

He found a branch hanging over the fence and dangled from it like a kid on the monkey bars. He shimmied across it and dropped down into the dark and empty (and probably haunted) cemetery. I copied his moves, step for step, and dropped in after him, checking over my shoulder every few seconds and listening carefully for nosey neighbors or pedestrians going for a late-night walk.

We ducked behind tall grave sites and monuments to avoid the spots of light dotting the cemetery from cars driving by and nearby houses. I followed him as we moved further into the cemetery and away from the fenced perimeter, staying low and in shadows. Dad wasn't saying anything. He wouldn't give me any specifics about what we were about to do, and it was driving me crazy.

But I guess I might be crazy, because I followed him without question.

Dad stopped at one of the less impressive gravestones. It was a flat, white stone slab that looked a hundred years old. The stone was cracked on one side and one of the corners had crumbled away.

"This is it."

"You say that like I know what we're doing here."

It was dark but I could still see Dad smiling at me. He surveyed the edges and checked over his shoulder for any midnight marauders—besides us, obviously. He went around to the corner opposite the collapsed edge and nudged it with his foot. It moved.

"I'm really not in the mood for seeing a corpse today. Just saying."

"Help me push this." He lowered to his knees and gripped the edge with his fingers. Together, we slid it across the lower slab, making a low crunching sound as the two pieces of stone were forced apart.

There was nobody inside—just an old set of stone stairs leading down into a pitch-black tunnel.

I looked at Dad. "Oh good. This just got scarier."

He winked at me and did a Scooby-Doo voice. "Ga-ga-ga-ga-ghosts!"

I had a flashlight and climbing gear but nothing for mummy, zombie, werewolf, vampire, demon or ghost hunting. When packing for a burglary, you never think, *Hmmm, do I need garlic cloves and a stake? Probably not.* And then you get into a situation like this.

I followed him down, bracing a hand against the damp stone wall as I moved carefully from one step to the next. Bits of loose rubble crumbled beneath my feet.

I bet there are, like, a million spiders on me right now.

"How exactly did you find out about this particular job?" I said, scratching my arm like a junkie, thinking about the bugs in the dirt around us.

Dad looked over his shoulder. "Audrey. Does it matter?"

"Yes. She hates me. And if Rhys finds out she's giving assignments to my *father*, he might do something idiotic, like ruin my life forever."

"He won't find out about me. I'm a little more careful about my real identity than you."

I gripped the damp wall. "How so?"

"For one, I'm not on Facebook." He stopped and considered for a second. "Actually, that alone makes up for a lot of it. You should be more careful."

"Says the guy leading me through an underground tunnel below a graveyard," I snapped.

"She just told me about this one because I live in the area and thought I could get to it before anyone else."

"Is there a chance someone else could be looking for it?"

"Yes."

"So, whatever it is that we're looking for might be gone already?"

"Yes."

"Oh good."

The ground felt moister as we moved further into the tunnel. The tunnel passageway narrowed and we had to turn sideways to get through. Wood beams that looked even older than the grave at the entrance braced the dirt ceiling of the tunnel. My back, knees and shoulders were caked with mud. And probably my ass—I could just tell.

It stinks down here. And I'm pretty sure I just stepped on a worm. I miss robbing rich people in nice houses.

"Speaking of relationships," I said, feeling a jagged rock scrape against my foot. "Why the hell are you seeing Audrey Fox? She's kind of awful."

"She's not so bad once you get to know her." He grinned. "I've always had a thing for powerful women, especially powerful, sexy British women."

"Ew. Thanks for that."

The tunnel widened as we reached the end, a blank wall staring back at us.

"Look. It's a *dead* end," Dad said, elbowing me and grinning like an idiot. "Get it? Dead end? 'Cause we're in a cemetery. D'ya get it?"

I shook my head. "This is no time for bad puns."

The round, underground room was likely sixteen feet at the widest point. I thought of the graves in the earth above us and shuddered. Dad ran his hand over the façade and looked around frantically, his flashlight flying as he searched for hints of a treasure.

"This isn't right," he said quietly. Maybe to himself, maybe to me, I'm not sure.

I ran my flashlight over the wall, looking for something. I had no idea what, though.

"What did Audrey say?"

"She told me where to find the grave and that's it."

"That's it? You didn't think to ask her for a little more information?"

"We were a little busy!" he snapped back.

I stared at him, disgusted by his candor. "Ew!"

He rolled his eyes and kept searching the muddy corners. I studied the smooth wall. I traced my fingers across it and felt a ridge. I poked my finger into the soft mud and hit something hard. I picked at it further and aimed the beam of my flashlight into the narrow hole I'd made. There was something silver in there and I kept clawing at it.

"If I dig into this wall, what are the chances of this whole tunnel caving in?"

"No idea," Dad said, holding up his flashlight so I could keep digging with both hands. "Keep going."

I found the edges of a silver-plated jar and scratched away the mud around it, carving it out of the soil. I was suddenly like Dr. Grant in that scene in the first part of *Jurassic Park*, except for the sweet hat and early '90s computer.

I slowly pulled the jar out and looked at the outside of it. Nothing was inscribed on the jar, but it certainly looked old. I picked mud from around the cap and twisted the top off. Dad aimed his flashlight inside.

"Nothing," he said. "Shit."

I looked inside. "Well, not *nothing*. There's some dust."

"That's not dust, punkin. That's an urn. Those are someone's ashes."

I am so totally gonna have a pissed-off ghost following me now.

"Oh, shit! Oh, gross! Ugh!"

I dropped the urn and it hit the ground with a clang. I stared down at it.

Why did that just clang?

I glanced at Dad and picked it up again. I turned on my flashlight and peered inside again. There was something glittering inside.

"I am so sorry, nameless dust person." I reached inside, cringing at the feeling of the remains on my skin. I looked at Dad again as my hand felt something smooth. I pulled my hand out of the urn.

I stared down at my hand. "That ... is a pretty nice necklace."

It was an antique choker-style necklace with diamond beading formed into a flower shape in the middle. Dust clung to every stone and every corner, but once cleaned up, it would fetch a healthy wad of cash.

Dad froze. "Someone's coming."

I heard the footsteps too. I slipped the necklace into my bra like a classy lady and dropped the urn again.

"Whoever you are in there, don't move," a man hollered from the shadows of the tunnel. "I'm just here for what's mine."

I know that voice.

"You stay where you are!" I yelled back. "There's nothing here for you!"

Dad looked at me like I lost my mind.

"Molly?" A form moved out from the shadows. "You've got to be kidding."

"Hello, Rhys."

His hair was a bit disheveled and his jeans and boots were covered in mud, but it was Rhys, no mistaking.

Dad looked at me, eyebrows up. Rhys gave him the once over.

"Molly Miranda Senior, I presume."

Dad didn't answer. At least he still didn't seem to know Dad's name specifically.

Rhys eyed the urn at my feet. "Oh, good. You've done the hard work for me already." He strolled over and picked it up, standing close to me, almost stepping on my feet. "Thanks, kid."

I stared him down.

He picked up the urn and turned it upside down, not taking his gaze off of me until all the dust slid out. I cringed.

At least that angry ghost is going to haunt Rhys now.

He glared at the pile of dust on the ground and sighed.

"Where is it?"

"Where's what?" Dad said.

"Don't play dumb. I'm really not in the mood." He looked back at me. "The necklace, where is it?"

"It's not here," I said. "Someone else got here before we did. The urn was already dug out when we got here."

"I don't believe you." He stepped close to me again and smiled. He leaned in close to whisper in my ear. "Where is it?"

"*Don't* touch her." Dad's eyes were flaming and his hands were curled into fists.

Rhys ignored him. "Where is the necklace, Molly?"

He grabbed my wrist. I slapped my other hand over his, twisted my wrist and pushed on his elbow, flipping him over onto the ground. I pinned him in place with my foot planted firmly on the side of his face.

Thanks, aikido self-defense training!

Rhys groaned into the mud and wiggled to get loose. He might have been a genius hacker but a fighter he was not.

"I don't have it." I said, still holding him tight while he squirmed. "It's gone. Now back the fuck off."

I looked at Dad. "Maybe we got the wrong grave."

Play along, Dad. Just do it.

"I don't know. That's just what he told me." He shrugged and looked genuinely pissed off. Having his daughter harassed right in front of him probably didn't help.

I lifted my foot and Rhys scrambled to his feet.

He rubbed his wrist and looked at me. "Who told you about the necklace?"

This time it was Dad who got to smirk. "I don't have to

tell you who I work for."

Rhys reached into his back pocket and aimed a pistol directly at my face.

"Yes. You do."

CHAPTER TEN

Life feels a bit different at the mouth of a pistol. It's funny what things pass through your mind.

My father is going to see his daughter get shot. That totally sucks. I'm a terrible person. I should have stayed in college. I should have gone skydiving while I had the chance. I should have gone swimming with dolphins. I should have seen The Spice Girls perform on their reunion tour!

"It is *far* too easy to buy a gun in this country," Rhys said, nearly doubled over with laughter. "God bless America!"

I glanced at Dad but didn't dare move. He looked tense but not scared or angry.

"Tell me who told you about the necklace or I'll shoot her."

Dad crossed his arms over his chest. "My guy is named Stan. He works out of Los Angeles. Now can you please lower your gun?"

Rhys's eye twitched. "Does Stan have a last name?"

"Stan doesn't give out his last name. He's a professional,"

Dad said. "Unlike some people."

If you hadn't noticed, Dad, there's a gun pointed at my head. Please don't be sarcastic.

"Stan from Los Angeles, you said?" Rhys thought for a moment, shrugged and put his gun away. "Well then. Guess I'm going to Los Angeles."

He headed out back down the tunnel and winked at me over his shoulder. "See you soon."

We waited a moment to say anything or move.

Dad cleared his throat. "Are you okay?"

I nodded, my heart still pounding. "I'm fine."

We squeezed back through the dank tunnel, peering out of the entrance to make sure the coast was clear. Then we climbed back over the fence and got in the car.

I closed my door and glared at Dad.

"What?"

"That's all you have to say?"

He started the car. "At least we got him out of our hair for a while."

"What happens when he can't find—" I did air quotes. "—Stan in Los Angeles? I'll tell you. He takes it out on me." I closed my eyes. "I'm finished."

"You're fine. Stan is a real guy."

"What?"

"He's an old business associate. Old-school mobster type." Dad stared at the road ahead of him. "I hope that little shit *does* find Stan and confronts him. Stan will have him killed. Maybe I should give him a heads up and let him know he should be expecting him—"

"I don't want Rhys murdered!"

"Why not?"

"Because I steal things from rich people. Murder's not really my scene."

"But it would solve all your problems. *And* he just pointed a gun at your head." He shrugged. "Even if it was just a fake."

I stared at him. "What did you just say?"

"Oh, that gun wasn't real. Plus, he wasn't even holding the damn thing right." He glanced at me. "You couldn't tell it was a fake?"

Oh. My. GOD.

"Not from where I was standing, no."

"You should brush up on your firearms knowledge, punkin. It's helpful to know."

"Thanks, I'll do that," I muttered.

"That creep may know a thing about hacking and burglary but he obviously doesn't know anything about guns or self-defense. You should have broken his arm. That would've been awesome."

I stretched the neckline of my shirt out in front of me and pulled the diamond necklace from my bra. The sharp edges of the stones had been poking me in the under-boob since we were in the tunnel. It was probably once draped around the neck of a very rich person or a celebrity or a Real Housewife of Key West. Even though it was covered in dust, it was quite unique and pretty. And by "dust," I mean remains.

Someone's ashes are in my bra. Oh my god, that is gross.

"What are you going to do with it?"

"It's yours," Dad said. "You're the one who found

the urn."

"Audrey told *you* about it, not me."

"I'm not taking it. You need the money. I don't."

"You heard Audrey," I said. "She can't have anything to do with me. I probably shouldn't even contact her again at this point. It's unsafe."

He sighed. "How about I sell it to Audrey for you? I'll wire you half of what I get and then invest the other half for you. She'll never even know you were involved."

"Rhys will somehow figure out we found that necklace." I assured him. "He always seems to just *know* what's going on with me."

"I'm trying to help you out, punkin. Do you need the money or not?"

I slumped down in my seat. "Fine."

Financially, I was not in a position to say no, but I still felt weird about it.

* * *

A few days later I packed my stuff back into the trunk of the rental car and hugged Dad goodbye.

"I wish you'd stay a little longer, punkin. It was nice having you around." He smiled and patted me on the back.

"Thanks for having me. It was nice being away from, well, everything. But I gotta go do a thing." I gave a weak smile. I wasn't very confident about it.

"Did you decide what you're going to do about your roommate?"

"No, not really. It would help if I knew how he

might respond."

"If it doesn't work out, you're always welcome back here. Just think of the all the grave-robbing adventures we could go on!"

I frowned at him. "I'd rather not do that again. Besides, Florida is … it's just not my style."

"The alligators aren't so bad. I mean, there is the occasional gun fanatic but…" He shrugged. "You could buy a mansion here for the amount you paid for that apartment. You should talk to that boyfriend of yours about moving down with you."

"I'm not doing that, Dad. And he's not my boyfriend."

He laughed. "I'm just teasing. You'll move elsewhere when you're good and ready."

We hugged and I drove home to New York.

* * *

A couple days later I was back in Manhattan, returning to a silent apartment.

When Nate finally got home late that night, dark shadows underlined his eyes. I looked up from my book and smiled as he slipped off his shoes. His mouth tightened when he saw me.

"Hi."

"You're back."

"Yeah."

Awkward silence. Cricket, cricket.

"There's some Chinese food in the fridge … if you're hungry," I said, trailing off at the end.

Oh my god, this is the worst.

"I'm fine." Nate stared at the wall.

He couldn't even look at me. This was going to be awful.

Nate got a bottle of water from the fridge—just one for himself. Usually he would ask me if I wanted anything while he was up. But I was no longer his concern. He sat down in the armchair across from me, instead of on the sofa beside me.

I was right. He hates me.

"How are you doing?" I forced a weak smile.

"Fine. Where did you jet off to this time?"

"Florida, to see my dad," I said. "And I didn't jet. I drove."

I intended to do this honesty thing the right way and keep it all legit.

I pulled my Betty Bruce passport from my back pocket, opened it to the page with my picture on it and held it up. "I want to talk about this."

Nate glanced at my passport. "Okay."

I really should have prepared a dramatic speech or something.

"Betty Bruce is the identity I use when I'm working. I use a fake name for safety reasons."

"You have a job?"

"Yeah. My parents don't actually own a ski resort. They didn't buy this apartment for me. I bought it myself."

"Jesus, what the hell do you do?" Nate's eyes grew wide.

Okay. You can do this. Just spit it out. One. Two. Three… No? Okay. You can just lie to him, you've gotten really good at it. It's fine. No. No! It's truth-tellin' time. He deserves to know the real you. Or does he? Maybe it's unsafe for him to know, especially with blackmailing jerks just running around. Yeah. That's it. I'm not telling him for his own safety! No! Just do it.

I cringed and finally pushed the words out. "I'm a professional thief."

His eyebrows went so high on his forehead, I thought they might leap off his face. "What?"

"People like having nice things that other people own. I'm hired to retrieve specific items in exchange for a fee. I deliver this item to my contractor. She gives the item to the client who requested it. I get paid."

"Are you serious?"

"Yes."

I bit my lip and watched his face slide back and forth between confusion, disbelief and dumbfounded blinking.

Nate sat back in the chair, staring straight ahead. "I thought you were an international escort or something. Or maybe a spy. I don't know."

"You thought I was a hooker?"

Spy, maybe. But prostitute?

"What kind of things do you steal?"

I suddenly felt like I was being interrogated on a bad police procedural.

"Historical artifacts, paintings, jewelry," I said. "Anything the client wants, really."

"Have you ever robbed a bank?"

I burst out laughing but stopped when I realized he was serious.

"No! I'm not a 1920s gangster. I mostly just steal from museums and private homes in Europe."

"Are you a kleptomaniac?"

"No."

He crossed his arms. "How much money do you make by stealing from people?"

"Like I said, I bought this apartment." I shrugged. "I'm doing alright, I'll put it that way."

His eyes were still wide. "Have you ever been caught?"

"Once, in college."

"You've been doing this *that* long?"

Longer, technically.

"Yes."

"Have you ever shot anyone?"

"No!" I blurted out, surprised he would even ask that. "I steal things. I would never intentionally hurt anyone." I looked straight at him. "I would never intentionally hurt *you*. I lied to you about a lot of things. And the only reason I'm telling you all of this now is because I care about you. I just ... please don't hate me."

"I don't hate you. I'm just not sure... It's a lot to process." He shifted in his chair, creases forming in his forehead as he thought hard about this whole new version of me. "Who else knows about ... your job?"

"My dad, the woman who hires me for assignments, the guy who used to hire me in New York when I first started out, Ruby—"

"*Ruby* knows?" Nate gestured wildly with his hands. "How did Ruby know before me?"

He might not know his cousin is a crooked accountant. I should probably keep my mouth shut.

"She's my best friend. Anyway, it's not exactly something I broadcast."

"You trust me to keep your secret?"

I nodded slowly. "And that's really something, 'cause I trust, like, hardly anyone."

Nate stood up and paced. "How do you know I won't tell the police?"

"I'll have to evict you if you do." I smiled but my grin quickly faded.

He's actually considering it.

"If you don't go to the police, I'll stop charging you rent," I said, my voice laced with desperation.

Nate looked really tense. He stuffed his hands in his pockets and leaned against the wall. "You're smart. I don't understand why you would get into that line of work anyway. How could you *possibly* think that was a good idea?"

"You want to be a comic book artist because you're *good* at it. Nate, I'm *really* good at this. Sometimes I think it's the *only* thing I'm good at—"

"Do *not* compare my life goal to what *you* do," he snapped. "You're a criminal. I don't even know who you are, but at least I know you're a criminal now." He shook his head and stared at the ceiling. "Fuck."

"It's just a job. It's not..." I cleared my throat, pushing past the aching spot near my larynx. "It's not who I am."

Nate thought for a minute. "I don't think I can stay here."

"Please—"

"I don't want to be here when police come through that door and ... something happens to you. What if you someday, I dunno, rob the wrong guy and he comes after you? What then?" His eyes met the floor.

"That's not going to happen," I said.

He nodded silently, staring at the wall behind my head.

Then he ducked into his bedroom and quickly appeared back in the hallway with an open gym bag, his laptop and toothbrush poking out beyond the zipper.

He'd already had a bag packed and ready to go. My throat tightened at the realization.

"I'm gonna stay at Logan's."

"Nate, please—"

"I can't stay here. I can't just sit here and watch you fuck up your life forever." He stole a single glance at me on his way out the front door.

* * *

A big cloud of sad hovered over me for the next few days. I didn't talk to anyone and I didn't go anywhere. I binged on Netflix and comfort food. After three days, Ruby forced her way in.

She cuddled in bed with me, cramming chips into her mouth.

"Nate's an idiot. Wow, your sheets are covered in chip crumbs. You know that, right?"

"He's not an idiot," I said, stuffing my face. "I'm the idiot."

She lifted up the sheet. "How did you even manage to get this many crumbs in here?"

"Maybe I should've just lied and said I was an escort. That's what he thought, anyway."

Ruby frowned. "He thought you were a hooker?"

I dropped my head back onto my pillow, exhausted. "Everything is so messed up, Ruby. The look on his face was just … awful. He probably hates me now. I don't know where my next job is coming from. Rhys probably wants to destroy me by now. My father is sleeping with Audrey—"

"What? *Ewwwwww!*"

"I know."

"Men are crazy." She brushed crumbs off my pillow and put her an arm around my shoulders. "I know a lot of lovely lesbians that would be happy to date a sexy, badass burglar chick. Do you want me to make some calls? I can get at *least* two of them over here right now if you want."

I smiled weakly. "No, that's okay. No matter what my grandmother said when I was a teenager, I'm pretty sure I'm straight."

Ruby eventually left me alone to wallow ("You're no fun. Are you sure you don't want to get high with me later?" "I'm fine, thanks."). Just me. Alone. Me and a bed covered in chip crumbs.

* * *

The next morning I opened my sleepy eyes, closed them again, wrapped the blankets tightly around me and rolled over. Unfortunately, I was already at the edge of the bed, so I dropped a foot and a half to the floor.

My bed is kicking me out. Even my mattress hates me.

In only underwear, I ate my cereal, surveying the world from the big living room window. I didn't have to worry about Nate startling me this time. I chewed slowly and didn't bother wiping excess milk from my chin.

It was two o'clock and I still hadn't showered. I just lay

on the couch and watched a *Judge Judy* marathon, silently criticizing the deadbeat boyfriends and fathers in my head.

"Yeah, you tell 'em, Judy," I said out loud.

You're losing it. Go take a shower. You know what you have to do to feel better.

* * *

Paul smiled when he saw me. The pawnshop was empty but Deanne gave me a quick hug, handed me a cookie and took Paul's spot at the front of the store while he and I had our grown-up talk in his office.

"How can I help you, young lady? Do you want a coffee?"

I smiled and shrugged. "No thanks. I was just checking in."

"Of course you were."

I grinned. Lying to Paul was like lying to my grandfather. Or Santa Claus.

I filled him in on the continuing saga of Rhys and his jackassery, including his ban on Audrey hiring me ever again.

"You need work?"

I nodded slowly, embarrassed to admit it.

Paul shuffled papers on his desk, quickly skimming over his messy, handwritten notes. Perhaps he was a doctor in a past life.

"What's your schedule like in the next few days?"

I smiled. "Wide open. What's up?"

"I may have something for you. You'll have to fly to Tulsa tomorrow."

Are you joking? I have to go all the way to Nebraska—

"Oklahoma."

"I knew that!"

I did not know that.

He slid a photo from underneath some papers and held it up. I looked at it then raised an eyebrow.

An Egyptian artifact with an enormous erection. Of course.

CHAPTER ELEVEN

Two days later, I was staring angrily at a map and hating my cell phone provider.

How could I possibly have had cell reception in Scotland but not in Oklahoma?

I tossed the map onto the bench beside me and looked around the truck stop restaurant. My fair skin probably set me apart from the tanned locals but no one asked me about my destination or where I was coming from. For now, I was safe.

I tried my phone again. No such luck. I grabbed the map again and squinted at the mass of tiny, intersecting lines. Naturally, Lake Virginia wasn't on the map.

Perhaps it should be called Pond Virginia. Or Puddle Virginia.

I wasn't sure exactly where I was on that map—somewhere on Highway 75, maybe—and I couldn't ask anyone either. That was a no-no. I could just picture some tobacco-chewing cowboy hauling up his britches and telling the local authorities, "Why yes, officer. I do remember talking to someone of that description. She was looking for Lake Virginia. Hey, she's not in any trouble, is she?"

I grabbed my big sunglasses from my bag and slid them on. My waitress, a Southern belle with big boobs and a lot of makeup, put my bill on the table and smiled.

"Are you sure I can't interest you in some dessert, honey? We got a whole *bunch* o' pies to choose from if y'all would like to see a menu."

Well, aren't you a walking stereotype?

I smiled weakly. "No. Thanks." I handed her cash. "Keep the change."

She glanced at the crumpled map. I should've put it away. "I'm just looking for the nearest town."

And by "nearest town," I, of course, mean where the fuck am I?

She stared at me wide-eyed, deer-in-headlights style.

"Ya know," I tried to help her out, "a town?"

"Agnes is about fifteen minutes east o' here. Where you headin'?"

Finally. Some good news.

"Dallas. Thanks."

Back in the car, I smiled as I put the key in the ignition. I was heading in the right direction. Before I left New York, I had Googled Lake Virginia, and Agnes was the closest town to it.

Now. If I can make it to a motel without getting attacked by a tornado, I'll be fine.

* * *

127

The booming metropolis of Agnes—insert sarcasm here—had three options for accommodations: a bed-and-breakfast, an RV park and a disgusting motel with hourly and nightly rates listed on the sign outside. I didn't have an RV, and B&B owners ask too many questions, so I checked into the disgusting motel on the edge of town, cursing Paul in my head.

To be fair, why should he waste an enjoyable, well-paid assignment on me? I deserted him for Audrey. I'm a sucky friend and Paul doesn't owe me anything.

The place was rank with the scent of cigarette smoke, even though it was a non-smoking room. I was too tired to care. I collapsed onto the hard bed, the springs creaking and clunking under my weight.

Usually this was the part where I would stare at the ceiling in an attempt to sleep. Instead I was staring back at myself.

There was a mirror mounted on the ceiling. Ew.

I feel like watching myself have sex would be distracting. I'd be all "What's going on with my facial expression right now?" and "Why does it look like I'm dying?" and "I didn't know my ass jiggled that much."

I slept for a few hours and then was back in action. I zipped up a black hooded sweatshirt and applied a generous layer of black face paint. (Balaclavas are stupid warm and they restrict your vision.) I put my suitcase, which held more gear than clothes, back in the car and headed for Lake Virginia.

It was shortly after midnight. That familiar feeling of adrenaline crept up on me. A smile spread across my face as I drove down a dirt road pointing me in the direction of the lake. This night's outing was just for surveillance purposes but I still twitched with anticipation.

I didn't know how many houses would be around the target's home—the road to Lake Virginia isn't on Google Maps. I didn't know who the target was or what his house looked like. Paul was a little vague on the details, almost certainly because the client was vague when describing where the item might be found. Sometimes a client might not know at all. It complicates things but it also increases the fee substantially.

The road continued on for a long ways, at least a few miles. There were no streetlights back here, just thick greenery on either side of the dirt road. There *were* power lines, so I knew there had to be something down there.

I kept my headlights dim. The moon was a sliver of light in the sky, always helpful when trying not to be seen.

The dirt road turned into a circular paved driveway with a closed gate. I turned the car around and drove back up the dirt road a ways, pulling off the side of the road as much as possible without actually going into the woods.

Nothing says suspicious like a car parked right outside your property. I was at least set up for a quick getaway if I needed one.

I couldn't see any cameras on the gate but I flipped my hoodie up just in case. The gate was wrought iron and pointy at the top. I went into the woods, where the gate was a bit lower and protected by overhanging trees. I scaled the gate with one foot on a tree and one on the metal bars of the gate, pulling myself up higher with an overhanging branch. I peered over the fence.

Virginia Lake wasn't wide but it was long. It stretched out ahead of me for what looked like miles, ending at a mountain range. The sky was wall-to-wall stars, and the calm water sparkled with their reflections. It was incredible.

"Wow," I whispered.

Security lights dotted a well-manicured lawn. A wooden dock bobbed gently on the lake. And tethered to that dock was a houseboat.

A fucking houseboat.

I've never stolen something from a houseboat before. Do they work like regular houses? What's the plumbing like in there? Does poo just go into the lake? Should I have packed a wetsuit? Do I even own a wetsuit? Where would I get a wetsuit around here? Can I swim with a hoodie on?

I lifted my binoculars and scoped it out.

Two stories high and bigger than most homes, the houseboat looked completely out of place in this woodsy, natural setting. The flat, fenced-in roof included a small sheltered area for a table and chairs. A set of golf clubs leaned against the table.

There's a driving range on that roof.

Besides the badass roof, the houseboat looked like a normal house with windows and wooden deck chairs outside the front door. I couldn't see a secondary entrance, and the windows were dark.

I looked around the property. The driveway was empty, which meant I probably had the place all to myself, maybe even for the whole night. I smiled and pulled on a pair of gloves. This surveillance mission had just turned into the real deal. If I could shave a day off this trip, the sooner I'd be home and the sooner I'd feel more secure about my finances, and my life in general.

I grabbed my gear from the car, shimmied up the fence from my spot by the tree and dropped down onto the property. Wind whistled through the trees and water sloshed against the sides of the houseboat. I took one last look around before approaching the dock.

I stepped as softly as I could but the boards creaked anyway. I didn't risk trying the front door in case there was an alarm system in place. I decided the best way in would be to climb up the side to the roof terrace and then go down from there.

Using the fence around the front door, I slowly found my footing and climbed up, each time checking the sturdiness of window frames before I put any weight on them. A piece of wood splintered beneath my fingertips and I breathed out a silent scream, my eyes welling with sharp, burning tears.

I reached the top, swung my legs over the side and avoided the driving range just in case I left footprints in the grass. A spiral wooden staircase led down to the second floor. I lay flat on my stomach and lowered my head over the side of the boat to see where the staircase ended. My stomach turned over in my gut.

The staircase ended right in front of a bedroom. Right beside the window was a bed. And in that bed was a man.

I whipped my head back up, my chest heaving and my pulse racing. I lay on the top deck, staying as still as I could.

Just walk away.

I lowered my head over the side once more, slower this time. The man was sleeping, his mouth stretched open like a hungry walrus. His chest rose then lowered slowly with each breath.

I'm sure if he were awake, he'd be out of bed calling the cops by now, not pretending to sleep.

I still couldn't risk going down the ladder in case he heard me, because he'd see me right away. Around the other side of the roof was a porch with a sitting area. I climbed down onto it and let myself in through the patio doors.

I can't just leave now. I came all this way. I'm already here. I might as well just find the statue and get the hell out.

Besides, I needed the money. This item didn't offer a huge payoff but at least it would hold me over for a few months. My bank account wasn't as amply stocked as I'd led my father to believe.

You'd be doing this anyway, even if you were chockablock with cash.

The place was dark inside. The stairs down to the main floor thankfully didn't creak as I stepped on each one, going slowly. The living room area was small with a sofa, a big armchair, a couple of bookshelves and a mantle over an electric fireplace. There were a few framed photos on the mantle, right next to the Egyptian artifact I had come to collect. About ten inches high, the statue looked extremely proud of his gigantic penis, which was at least four or five inches long. He was smiling. Ew.

Who would keep this thing next to photos of their children?

I reached for the statue. Before I could decide how to get off the houseboat, there was a loud bang, followed by the big front window shattering from top to bottom. Thousands of shards of glass fell everywhere.

There is no way the guy upstairs didn't hear that. Shit.

A tall, dark figure stood on the patio, pointing a gun straight at me. I dropped the statue and threw myself behind the couch, covering my face to avoid the layer of glass on the carpet.

The guy upstairs was yelling but I couldn't make out what he said over the high-pitched ringing in my ears caused by the gunshot.

He appeared at the top of the stairs, a phone in his hand. "I'm calling the cops!"

Before he finished dialing the number, the gunman aimed the gun at his chest and shot twice. The man's body fell back limply and crumpled to the floor. The wall was dotted with blood behind him, and a red stream trickled down onto the floor below the open stair steps.

I turned and stared at the gunman, my eyes wide. "What do you want?" I grabbed the Egyptian statue. "This?"

The gunman nodded. I slowly passed the statue to him. It was dark but I could see he was wearing a balaclava. The gunman looked at the statue for a second and then aimed the gun at my forehead, touching the nozzle to my bangs.

"Oh god. Please don't kill me," I whispered, closing my eyes.

This is it.

Silence.

I opened one eye. The gunman checked the chamber and grunted in frustration.

His gun is jammed. Oh my god, his gun is jammed!

The gunman pistol-whipped me across the face and I fell backwards to the floor, nearly cracking the back of my head on the electric fireplace. I wiped a few drops of blood away from my eye, the socket aching.

The gunman took off, running down the dock at high speed. He jumped off the dock and dove into the water, graceful and fast, and swam towards the other side of the lake.

I gotta get out of here.

I pushed myself off the carpet and bolted out of the houseboat, leaping over the broken window. I just stared straight ahead at the wooded area I come in through. I ran so hard and so fast, my legs burned.

Ya know, I wish people would stop pointing guns at me. Enough is enough!

I threw myself into the trees, climbed the gate, jumped down and got in the car. I didn't look back. I thought my heart might explode as I sped down the dark road, much faster than I should. I needed to get off this road as soon as possible, before the police showed up.

What if the police stop me on my way back into town? I'm wearing black face paint and dressed all in black. That's *not suspicious at all.*

This thought made me drive even faster. I slowed down as soon as I saw headlights from other vehicles and then sped back up again when they disappeared from my rear-view mirror.

I never thought I'd be so happy to see that dingy motel again. I parked the car, unlocked the room door and looked over my shoulder. Luckily for me, the place was a ghost town. I went inside and closed the curtains.

I raced to the bathroom and heaved into the toilet, my fingers gripping the seat. My whole body lurched and spasmed with every wave of sickness that crashed into me.

Once my stomach had emptied, I stood up and washed

my face. Beneath that black makeup, my face was snow white. I washed away all black smudges of face paint from the sink. A hard, tight ball formed in my throat.

I cannot fucking cry right now. Not now. No way. Stop being such a pussy.

I stood by the window for an hour, peeking out from behind the curtain. I eventually sat down on the floor and watched as a few cars drove by. The same thoughts kept running through my head.

Someone tried to shoot me. Someone wants me dead. Who would want that? Who knew I would be at that location tonight?

I fell asleep on the floor by the window when the sun was just rising up over the hill. It wasn't what you'd call a restful sleep.

When I woke up I checked the local news and listened to the radio. There was no mention of the shooting or the break-in. I booked a flight back to New York and left the motel before six in the morning. I drove by a cop car on the way to the highway but just avoided eye contact and kept driving. I found a park in a suburb of Tulsa and sat in my car for a few minutes, just staring at a pay phone near the parking lot.

Oh my god. Pay phones are still a thing?

I slid my hands into a pair of thick latex gloves, pulled on a baseball cap and walked over to the pay phone. I looked over my shoulder. It was early but a few people were milling around the park in the distance. I lifted the receiver, slid a coin into the slot and dialed 9-1-1. I looked over my shoulder again.

"Nine-one-one. What is your emergency?"

I lowered my voice. "Man shot in a houseboat on Lake Virginia near Agnes."

I hung up as fast as I could and got back in my car. I threw the baseball cap on the passenger seat and drove away before anyone saw me.

Why did I just do that? That dude was not my problem.

But I couldn't help but feel like he would still be alive if it weren't for me. That man had a family. What if they showed up at the houseboat in a few days? What if one of his kids discovered his bloody, rotting body instead of the police? What if animals snacked on his body and his kids saw? His family didn't deserve that.

I was still incredibly stressed out and twitchy when I arrived at the airport. I forced myself to stop tapping my foot as I waited for my flight. Nobody gave me a second glance or asked me any questions when I went through security. Nothing.

I checked the news sites on my phone again, even checking the local police Twitter feed. Again, there was no mention of a murder or a break-in. It didn't calm me down in the least.

The empty waiting area started to fill as the departure time drew near. Someone dropped a black backpack into the seat next to me. The owner of the backpack sat down on the other side.

"It's funny how we keep running into one another," said a man with a Scottish accent.

I slowly moved my eyes to the right, just to confirm my suspicions.

It was Rhys.

CHAPTER TWELVE

I flopped down into the seat by the window.

"That's actually *my* seat by the window." Rhys sat in the seat beside me on the plane. "But you can have it. I'm just that thoughtful."

"You're a saint," I said flatly.

Rhys ignored my comment and looked around the plane. "Where's the stewardess? I need a drink."

"Flight attendant. Can't you wait until we're in the air?"

"I could." He shrugged. "But I don't want to."

"How is it that you managed to be on the exact same flight as me?" I kept my voice low.

"I get a notification on my phone whenever you book a flight online." Rhys was still peering anxiously around the plane. "I was just in California, as you may have known, so I made sure to get a connecting flight in Tulsa to New York on my way back home."

Dad would be disappointed to hear Rhys hadn't been

killed and buried in a ditch somewhere.

"You couldn't afford a direct flight from L.A.?"

"Oh, I absolutely could. But where's the fun in that?"

Rhys fixed his flights just so he could be at the airport in Tulsa to see me? I call bullshit. He must have another reason for being here...
Oh my god.

It was Rhys. Rhys was the one who shot that guy last night! And then he tried to shoot me!

I swallowed hard and stared out the window, my stomach aching. My hands shook so I slipped them into the front pocket of my hoodie before he could see.

Once the plane was in the air, I got a tiny bottle of liquor and downed it fast. Rhys sipped a glass of whiskey, looking as cool as a cucumber. He eyed the tiny, empty bottle and glanced at me.

"Since when are you a nervous flyer?"

"The last time I saw you, you pointed a gun at me," I whispered.

Rhys rolled his eyes. "It wasn't a real gun."

The gun was definitely real. It broke a window. An innocent man is dead. I saw it!

"Your dad's little wild goose chase was so much fun, by the way. Some thugs laughed at me when I asked to speak with Stan. But then I hung out on the beach and fucked a surfer girl, so it wasn't a total loss."

He's not talking about last night. He's talking about what happened in the tunnel in Key West.

"It certainly felt real," I said.

"I hope you know I would never actually shoot you. I just wanted—" He lowered his voice "—the item. It's not a big deal." He finished off his whiskey.

"You're lucky my dad didn't put out a hit on you."

That may have been the tiny bottle talking.

"He has that kind of power, huh?" He nodded, looking impressed. "It's cute that you're trying to follow in his footsteps."

"That's not what I'm doing."

Rhys tilted his glass back and forth so the ice slid from one side to the other. He was slouched low in his seat so our faces were at the same height. It was a little more intimate than I would prefer. I took out a novel I bought at the airport and pretended to be interested in reading it.

"Don't you want to know why I would never kill you?"

"Because then you wouldn't have me to stalk online or torment on long plane trips."

"No. Although, now that you mention it, that *is* an added bonus." He grinned and winked. "No, I've decided you could be useful."

I rolled my eyes. "What?"

"I want to start my own agency. And I want you to work for me."

"No thanks."

"You're really good at this. It comes naturally to you. I mean that in the most complimentary way. And I promise, I would pay better than Paul."

Of course *he knows I'm working for Paul. Is there anything about me he doesn't already know?*

"Working for Paul is fine. I sure wish Audrey was allowed to hire me, though." I glared at him.

"Ah, yes. That." He frowned. "Well, Casey is proving to

be … not a great fit."

I avoided making conversation for the next half hour. Instead, I drank. After several tiny bottles of alcohol, I became chattier.

"I've been thinking about quitting."

Rhys, now on his third whiskey, shook his head. "Don't be ridiculous."

"No, it's true. Nate knows what I do and now he hates me."

"Ah yes. Your roommate? Is he your—" Rhys closed his eyes for dramatic effect "—*lover?*"

"Former roommate. I guess I can't really blame him. He's too good for me." I shrugged and leaned up against Rhys's shoulder, my head resting against his head.

Why did I start drinking? I cannot be so familiar with someone who tried to kill me last night. Now, where is that flight attendant? I need another tiny bottle of alcohol.

"He's obviously a fool," he mumbled.

"You don't even know him," I mumbled back.

Rhys pointed at me, his finger hovering uncomfortably close to my boob. "If he cannot accept who you are as a person, who you are inside, then fuck 'im."

"I already did that." I paused. "Oh, you mean forget him. I can't do that. Quitting is easier than just giving up on him."

"Have you even ever *had* a normal job?"

I snorted. "No."

"Well, good luck with that. Let me know how that goes. He must be pretty special."

"Things have been shitty recently," I said. "I mean, last night was just a mess."

"Yeah, what were you doing in Tulsa anyway?"

I looked straight at Rhys's face. He seemed genuinely interested. Even if my sober self hadn't come to terms with it, my drunk brain knew it—Rhys wasn't at the houseboat the night before. He hadn't tried to kill me. In fact, he honestly seemed to know nothing about the incident.

Plus, Rhys is an inch shy of six feet tall. The gunman from the night before was closer to five eight.

"Visiting a friend." I glanced at him, suddenly a bit sleepy.

I stared out the window, contemplating how my life had turned out this way. Some of my friends in high school had gone on to become functioning members of society. They all seemed generally happy for choosing that path. Why wasn't that good enough for me?

"What was your first job assignment?" I said, still staring out the window.

"My old boss sent me to Wales to acquire a letter from an old lady's home. She lived all alone in this big old house in the country. She had no security system whatsoever and didn't even lock her windows at night." He stared ahead as he recalled the memory. "I just walked right in while she was asleep in her chair, found the letter and walked out. I don't even know if she knows it's missing to this day."

"What was in the letter?"

"A rather risqué piece of mail from a woman who is now married to a Member of Parliament. Turns out she and this old lady used to be lovers." He smiled. "The letter was very sweet... A little more explicit than I expected but kind of funny, really."

I giggled quietly and wiped my weary eyes.

"What about you? What was your first assignment?"

"Another time maybe," I whispered. "I'm sleepy."

I fell asleep on Rhys's shoulder, only waking up when we reached New York. I sat up quickly and pretended I hadn't just been drooling on his collar. A throbbing headache had planted itself firmly on my left temple.

I got off the plane without a word to Rhys and was quickly heading for the exit when he caught up to me and grabbed my hand.

"Wait," he said. "I have a few hours before my connection to Glasgow. Why don't we get a drink at the bar?"

"I think I've had enough for today. My head is killing me. I gotta get home."

"Can I come?"

"Excuse me?" I stared at him.

Rhys shrugged. "I have some time to kill."

"You're not coming to my house."

"I thought we had nice talk—"

"I was drunk. I don't even remember most of what I said."

Liar.

"Besides," I said. "You and me? We are not friends."

"What? Why not?"

My eyes widened. "Oh, I don't know! How about the—" I lowered my voice "—blackmail? How about putting a gun to my head and threatening to kill me in Florida? Ring any bells?"

Rhys frowned and furrowed his brow. I didn't wait for him to think of a response and continued towards the exit.

"Alright. I guess this is goodbye then," he said loudly.

I looked back at him.

"You're quitting. Remember?" He crossed his arms over his chest.

"Booze makes me overdramatic. I don't know what I'm doing yet. Except leaving this airport and going home."

Rhys opened his arms up to hug me.

"What are you doing?"

"Come 'ere."

"No."

"Molly. Come here."

"No! Put your goddamn arms down!" I hissed.

"Please don't make a scene."

I glanced around. People were starting to stare at us. I glared at him, put my suitcase down and quickly patted him on the back, my arms around his ribs.

"See, was that so hard?"

"Don't talk to me. You smell like whiskey."

He laughed and headed back into the airport. "I'll see you 'round, kid."

"No, you won't."

"Oh, yes I will!" he shouted before disappearing down a hallway.

I really hate that guy.

* * *

Paul folded his hands on his desk and stared at the window.

"I'm so sorry I let you down."

He waved his hand. "It's alright. You coulda been killed. I mean, obviously, I'm not thrilled at how this turned out but I'm glad you didn't get hurt." He slurped his coffee.

"And you're sure you didn't see the guy's face?"

I shook my head. "It all happened so fast."

"That artifact is basically useless now. Not a lot of people want to suspiciously acquire an item when the original owner has recently been murdered," Paul mumbled. "What a waste."

"What happened? Why would another thief have even been there?"

He sighed. "It sounds like it was a double booking."

I stared at him. "You think that's what happened here?"

Sometimes a client will hire a second consultant because they want to make sure the job gets done. Whichever consultant gets the item first gets the reward money. I hate when clients do that. It's a shitty thing to do. That's how people get hurt.

"Your competition broke the rules. I know this wasn't your fault, missy. Just let me sit on this for a while. For all we know, someone is still looking for you. Might be too early to send you back into the wilds just yet."

"Yeah. I guess."

"I'll give you a call in a few weeks. We'll see where we are then."

Paul patted me on the shoulder and smiled as I left the pawnshop.

Great. I'm losing out on even more money.

I messed up. I should have scoped the place out more before I went in. I should have been more careful.

Maybe I'm not cut out for this.

* * *

Ruby, wine glass in hand, stretched out her legs and rested her bare feet on her coffee table, wiggling her toes as she sipped.

"What'd Paul say?"

"He's disappointed. It'd be better if he just got angry with me."

Ruby handed me the wine glass and I took a gulp.

"This wine is terrible." I took a second gulp and handed it back to her.

"It does the trick, though, doesn't it?"

I shrugged. "I guess." I burped and slouched down into the couch cushions. All I wanted was to put on pajamas and watch TV for the rest of my life. Instead I was wearing sparkly flats and a black party dress that Ruby told me to put on. She was wearing a pink dress thing that could probably pass for lingerie. She made it look like couture.

"I can't believe you're dragging me out when I'm feeling this shitty."

"This place is fantastic. You will have an awesome time, I promise."

I fucking doubt it.

We finished getting ready and took a cab to a club in Brooklyn. It just looked like an abandoned warehouse on the outside, a line of smartly dressed ladies and gents waiting to get inside. The bouncer at the entrance looked about six feet wide at the shoulders. As soon as he saw us, Ruby kissed him on the cheek and he raised the barrier rope for us.

I looked at Ruby, my eyebrows up.

"His boss is a client." She winked, grabbed my hand

and we went inside.

I've never been one of those girls who enjoy clubbing. I knew immediately this place wasn't for me when I heard a dance remix of a Rihanna song blasting. There were flashing lights and glow sticks and *so many* sweaty people and drinks being spilled on the dance floor.

I looked at Ruby. "Can I go home now?"

"Don't be such a baby." She grabbed my hand and pulled me further in. We pushed past people dancing and got a couple drinks, then went upstairs to the balcony and found an empty spot next to a few people.

One of them grabbed Ruby, screamed like a teenage girl and hugged her tight. "Ohmygawd, you made it!"

A guy in the same group hugged Ruby and kissed her on the cheek. "What the fuck are you wearing? It's disgusting. I fucking love it!" He hugged her again and spotted me. "Oh, hi. Who's this?"

Ruby, the social butterfly, was in her element. "This is Molly. She's my bestie. Molly, this is Silas." She pointed to the other two in the group. "And that's Fawn and that's Tegan."

Silas, Fawn and Tegan. Where do these people even come *from?*

Her friends were so hip. I waved awkwardly and tugged at the bottom of my dress to cover more thigh. I felt naked, even though there were lots of people here less covered.

The song changed and the whole group, except me, screamed and jumped up.

"This is my jam!" Fawn shouted.

I can't believe she just said that.

Ruby leaned in close to me. "We're gonna go dance. Do you want to come with us?"

I shook my head and nodded to my cocktail. "Maybe later."

Ruby, Fawn and Silas rushed downstairs. I watched them over the guardrail of the balcony. This was *so* not my scene.

"I love your freckles," Tegan said, sliding over on the couch. "What did you say your name was?"

"Molly." I smiled and sipped my drink.

I wonder how early I can get out of here without seeming like a complete loser.

Tegan crossed her long legs and fiddled with her phone. I'm not sure how she even crossed her legs while wearing leather pants that tight. She sipped her drink, stood up and watched our friends dancing on the floor below.

"Ruby is so much fun."

"Yeah. She's a good friend." I shrugged. "This isn't really my thing. She kind of dragged me out here."

She turned around to face me and leaned her elbow against the railing. "This music is so cheesy. I prefer something with a little more of an edge." Stray pieces of her short black hair fell in front of her dark eyes.

I nodded. "Yeah, me too."

I stood up to watch our friends, finishing off my drink with one swig.

"I know a club a few blocks from here," Tegan said, slipping her hand around my hip. "Why don't we go check it out?"

A lot of Ruby's friends are gay and bisexual, and I hang out with her revolving door of fabulous friends a lot, but none of them had ever hit on me before.

"Um, no thanks. I think I'd better stay here. Unless

Ruby wants to go—"

Tegan stepped closer to me. "Come on. Let's ditch 'em. We could have some fun." She raised an eyebrow.

I was feeling pretty tipsy but not quite tipsy enough to start batting for the other side. This chick was certainly hot but just not my type. That is to say, she wasn't a dude.

I held up my empty glass. "I'm gonna go get another drink."

I shuffled my way through the people downstairs, the music pumping so loudly I could feel it in my chest, and made it to the bar. I ordered two long tubes of lime green something—not even sure what it was—and downed them fast.

If I'm going to actually have fun tonight, I'd better drink up.
And I did.

I pushed my way through the crowd again and found Ruby and her friends. I let the combination of liquor and remixed Britney Spears take me away in its late-night, techno-drenched arms.

I was dancing close to Silas when Ruby grabbed my hand and pointed across the bustling dance floor.

It was Nate. I stopped dancing and just stared at him. I couldn't even tell you what song was playing at this point. Everything just went blank.

Ruby looked back at me. Silas shrugged and went off to dance with a shirtless guy nearby. She pulled me aside.

"Are you gonna go talk to him?"

I nodded, my head heavy.

"How drunk are you?"

I nodded again.

"Good. You're ready," she said, giving me a not-so-gentle push in Nate's direction.

I wove in between people and found him standing with his friends. He was holding a beer and already had a rosy shine to the top of his cheeks. He was laughing hard at something someone said.

He's drunk too. Awesome. It was meant to be.

He spotted me and the smile tumbled from his face. He glanced at his friends and they went off towards the bar. I stood in front of him, giving a shy wave. It seemed the better option between that and screaming "I am so uncomfortable!" directly into his ear.

"How are you?" he asked, shifting his feet.

"I'm good."

Liar.

"Are you having a good time? This isn't really your kind of place." He sipped his beer.

"Ruby persuaded me. It's not really your kind of place either."

He chuckled. "Logan peer-pressured me."

I nodded.

This is so awkward.

He put his empty beer bottle on a nearby table. "Do you want to dance?"

I nodded. He took my hand and led me to the dance floor, crammed with drunk twenty-somethings and smelling of Axe body spray, perfume and sweat. It was less than romantic. We danced close together. I felt his breath on my cheek and then his lips on my neck. I pulled him closer and kissed his mouth. He was delicious, a magical mixture of liquor and whatever spectacular ingredient makes Nate the man he is.

Ruby, also pretty drunk now, squealed when she saw us. "Ew! I don't want to see my cousin making out with my friend!"

I laughed and Nate blushed. He lowered his mouth to my ear.

"Come home with me."

"To our apartment?"

"No. I don't live there."

That's right. He doesn't live with me anymore.

"I moved into a new place yesterday." He kissed my cheek and repeated, "Come home with me."

We bolted out of there, hailed a cab and attacked one another in the back seat. The driver hummed along with his radio and ignored us. Drunken make-outs in the back of his car were probably pretty common.

I pawed at his chest and kissed him passionately. (Nate, not the taxi driver.) Nate's hands were all over me. His glasses started fogging up and I giggled like a hyena.

Nate's new apartment was on a sketchy street in Brooklyn, not far from the club. It was a basement bachelor apartment with metal bars on the one single window. It couldn't have been more than 200 square feet. Cardboard boxes were piled high along one wall.

He threw his keys down on a nearby table and scratched the back of his neck. "This is home. I haven't finished unpacking yet."

The floor was brown carpet, with multiple stains. The walls were burnt orange and cracked from ceiling to floor. The bathroom, although I didn't look inside, looked barely big enough for a toilet and a sink, let alone a shower. There was certainly no king-size luxury tub, like at my apartment.

This is what minimum wage looks like. This is what I'm missing out on.

Nate put his arms around me and kissed my neck. "I've missed you," he whispered.

I was frozen. The drunk part of me wanted to push Nate onto that twin size bed in the corner and make muskrat love. But the sober part of me was suddenly very aware of what my life could be like if I decided to change things.

It was a strange feeling.

"I can't do this."

He looked down at me, eyebrows raised. "Is something wrong?"

My tubes of alcohol were wearing off but Nate was still intoxicated.

I didn't want to tell him the truth, that I was scared to death of the possibility of having a normal, regular person's life. I'd gotten so comfortable in my weird world that clean money just became this theoretical idea and not a physical item.

Unless my luck doesn't turn around soon. Then I'm going to have no other choice.

"I feel nauseous." I felt fine but I didn't want to hurt his feelings.

Nate got me a glass of water. We curled up in his tiny bed and watched some terrible kung fu movie on TV then fell asleep together like spoons.

It was around ten when I woke up to the sound of my phone ringing. I was just going to let it go to voice mail, but whoever was calling me kept hitting redial.

Nate stumbled off the bed and handed it to me, looking like he was in hangover-induced agony. He groaned and put the pillow over his head.

Caller ID let me know it was one of the many people I had no interest in talking to at the moment—Audrey Fox.

I put the phone to my cheek. "What could you *possibly* want?"

"I thought you should know Paul was shot last night."

CHAPTER THIRTEEN

I paced my apartment. Two hours had passed since Audrey called me to tell me Paul was shot. I didn't know if he was alive or dead.

"Don't do anything stupid like go to the hospital," she had said. "I'll call you when I have more information."

Nate offered to make me breakfast but I got out of there as fast as my sparkle-covered flats could carry me.

You know what's fun? Not having sex but still having to do the walk of shame in a party dress on the subway the next morning.

Not knowing Paul's condition was horrible. I considered using a fake name (and a fake voice but that didn't seem necessary after I thought about it) and calling the hospital to enquire but decided against it.

Audrey finally contacted me after lunch. "Paul's wife just called me from a pay phone. He's out of surgery and resting now. They don't know who shot him but they're hoping to get something from him once he wakes up," she said. "*Don't* go to the hospital."

"What is Deanne's number? I'm going to call her—"

"Do not call them. Are you stupid? The police will be watching their every move for a while. You will not call them and you will not go to the hospital, do you understand?"

As much as I hated to admit it, she was right. It was too risky.

Could it be the same person who tried to kill me in Oklahoma? Paul must have enemies. It might not be related to me at all.

But what if it is?

The thought was agonizing and it kept running around my head, over and over. Sitting around my apartment and staring at the walls wasn't helping. I got changed and headed to the gym in the basement.

I attacked the punching bag with every inch of energy I had, although my hangover held me back substantially. A terrible ache formed in my gut. I wanted to call Dad and tell him but didn't want Audrey to get a busy signal. There was a chance Audrey had told him anyway.

What if Paul dies because of my *fuck-up?*

I pounded harder on the punching bag. My knuckles were starting to hurt within my thick gloves and my upper arms were burning.

What happened in Oklahoma was not entirely my fault. I could've been in and out in minutes. Why would someone want to kill me? And who would know where I was at that exact moment?

There was a possibility that it was, in fact, another burglar who was assigned the job and they just didn't know what they were doing. It could have been a rival burglar who wanted to scare off a competitor for the job.

No. They weren't just trying to scare me off. That person wanted me dead. They were likely frustrated—furious, even. But why shoot Paul?

What if they are trying to lure me to the hospital so they can try to shoot me again? I don't even know if it was a man or a woman.

I jogged back to my apartment, using the stairwell instead of the elevator.

What, is there a bomb attached to the elevator now? Stop being an idiot. No one would go through that much effort. You're not that interesting.

After a quick look around in my apartment—all clear—I locked my front door and checked all the locks on my windows.

The mystery gunman didn't hit me with a bullet but he certainly hit me with fear and paranoia.

My phone beeped and I jumped out of my skin. It was a text from Nate.

Nate: *Is everything all right? You seemed weird this morning.*

I hesitated. Telling him the truth might scare him off.

Molly: *Something happened to a co-worker, I'm just waiting to hear back. I'm sorry I had to run out this morning. That was not the plan originally, I swear.*

Nate: *That's OK. I get off work at 7. Can I come over after?*

Molly: *Sure.*

* * *

Nate showed up at my door with a six-pack of my favorite beer.

"What a gentleman," I said, closing the door behind him.

"Not a problem." He cracked one open for me and one for himself, storing the rest in the fridge.

We sat in our usual spots on the sofa, enjoying a moment of comfortable silence.

"So, what happened to your co-worker?" Nate said.

"I'd rather not talk about it." I wrinkled my nose. "How's work?"

"It's fine." He hesitated for a moment. "Someone at the restaurant has a friend who works at an office and he said they are looking for someone to fill a junior position right away..."

I sipped my beer. "But what about the restaurant and your comic book stuff?"

The corner of Nate's mouth curled into a shy smile. "Not for me. For you."

I stared at him and did my best not to burst out laughing.

You want me to take a shitty minimum wage job in some shitty office where I'd work with shitty people and, like, shitty staplers?

"I have this apartment to pay for," I tried to reason, "I can't just go from what I make now to a minimum wage job. I just can't. It's not that simple."

Just as I was reaching over to put my beer on the coffee table, there was a loud thud from the hallway—probably someone slamming a door. I dropped the beer to the floor and it shattered, spraying foam and beer.

"Whoa," Nate said. "Are you alright?"

I chuckled. "Yeah! I'm just klutzy."

"Your hands are shaking."

I held my hands tight in my lap to force the quivering to stop. "No, they're not. I'm fine."

"Molly, are you alright?"

I honestly don't know.

Nate helped me clean up the mess. We chatted a bit then he headed out. He was just about out the door when I stopped him.

"Wait, Nate." I sighed, hesitating and feeling like a coward. "Can you text me your friend's number? I'd like to talk to him a little bit about the job."

Nate smiled. He wrapped his arms around me and squeezed me tight, kissing me on the cheek. "I'll let him know you're interested. Thanks for giving it a chance."

I closed the door behind him. I leaned my forehead against it and pounded it softly.

Are you happy, Universe? You win.

* * *

"Hi there! You must be Meagan! I'm Brenda. So nice to meet you. Have you ever worked in an office environment before? Anything in customer service?"

I stared blankly at the cheerful woman behind the desk. We were in a tight cubicle with three walls. The whole floor of this office building smelled like carpet. The *tap-tip-tap* of keyboards overpowered any other sound, even ringing phones and low chatter.

More importantly, I was wearing a suit. A *suit*.

Nate had suggested I wear one. I originally bought it for a funeral four years ago and had to brush the dust off the shoulders. It was a little tight around the upper arms but it was good enough for today.

"It's Molly," I said quietly. "And no, I've never worked

in an office before."

Brenda got that "Oh, shit, another newbie" look on her face but it quickly switched back to exaggerated friendliness.

"Pardon me. It says Meagan on your form." She frowned and jotted something on the paper. "Are you familiar with Microsoft Office?"

No.

"Of course." I smiled wide.

"Do you have any other skills that might be useful in an office environment?"

No.

"I'm a team player." I swallowed.

Fuckfuckfuckfuck. What else did that employment website say?

"I'm also … motivated." I nodded. "And I'm, um, a good listener and a good, um … communicator." I swallowed again. My throat felt like sandpaper.

I can also climb most buildings with relative ease, break into a safe and tell a real diamond from a fake one.

"There's no need to be nervous, Meagan. This isn't an interview. I'm just figuring out how much training you will need."

I smiled weakly.

"Now, you'll be doing chat support on our website. When people have a problem with one of our many office supply products, they go to the chat box and speak directly with us."

Are you joking? That's a job? My job?

"What kind of problems?"

"Oh, you know. The usual." Brenda counted on her

fingers. "What should I do if my stapler is jammed? My hole punch broke before the warranty was up. Can I get a refund? What should I do if I accidentally eat an eraser? That sort of thing." I opened my mouth to ask her if a lot of people eat erasers but she kept talking. "Once you're here for a year or two, then we will likely consider you for a sales position." She beamed. "I'm going to put you in a cubicle with Allie. She's great. You'll love her."

"Great," I said, almost whispering.

I followed Brenda to a cubicle on the far right. All the big windows were on the left. Instead of a view of the ugly building beside this one, I got a gray wall.

Allie was typing at her computer with headphones on. She slid them off and gave me a once-over before giving a little wave.

"Hi. I'm Allie. Nice to meet you."

"I trust you can show Meagan the ropes?" Brenda scurried away before Allie could answer.

I put my purse on the empty desk across from her. It was so cramped in this cubicle with two desks.

Allie looked over her shoulder. "Did she give you any account info?"

"No."

"Well, you'll need account info before logging in." Allie put her headphones back on.

I sat in my chair and turned on my computer. As expected, it asked for login info. I tapped Allie on the shoulder.

"Uh ... who do I talk to about getting—"

"You'll have to get that from Derek." She turned back to her computer.

I stared back at the computer screen. I felt like an idiot. I cleared my throat. "Who is Derek?"

"The IT guy."

I walked back to Brenda's desk.

"Sorry to bother you. Allie told me I need to talk to Derek about getting login info for my computer...?"

"Oh. He's on vacation for a couple days. We'll have an account set up for you when he gets back." Brenda turned back to her computer and kept working.

"Is there something I should be doing until then?" The words were barely above a mousey squeak.

Brenda thought for a moment. "Do you know how to use a shredder?"

I didn't. Brenda showed me how, seeming less friendly with every passing moment.

I stood in the supply room, shredding documents for the rest of the morning. After two hours of shredding, it was hypnotic. The sound of the machine chewing the paper fibers and spitting them out. The hum of the fluorescent lights. The soft crunch made by the shreds when I pushed them further down into the garbage to make room for more. Since I didn't have to focus on the task at hand, my mind was free to wander to happier places. Family vacations with Mom, my sister and, occasionally, my dad. Joyriding in my car instead of attending geography class on a Friday during my senior year. Stealing a stupidly huge diamond necklace from a Connecticut mansion three years ago. I also thought about Paul in the hospital and how, if he died, I would never forgive myself.

Nate texted me at 11:30. Nobody was around so I took

a break to check it.

Nate: *How's your first day so far?*

Molly: *Fine.*

Nate: *Yeah?*

Molly: *I now know how to use a paper shredder. My life is complete.*

By noon I'd barely made a dent in the pile. Nate offered to meet me for a quick lunch in the crowded cafeteria on the main floor of the building.

"I wish you had longer for lunch," I said, picking at a chocolate chip muffin.

"Usually I don't get a lunch break until around two. 'Cause, you know, lunch is when people go to restaurants, to have lunch. Bastards."

He was trying to make me smile. I wasn't in the mood. "You look sad."

I shrugged. "I just have a headache. I think it's the fluorescent lighting."

It certainly has nothing to do with this awful, boring, stupid, pointless, mundane and depressing job. I doubt my paycheck will even cover my phone bill.

"Did you hear about your co-worker yet?"

I shook my head. Paul was still in a coma. His doctors had expected him to be awake hours after surgery. Hours had turned into days.

"Since you're not telling me about the friend," Nate lowered his voice, "I assume something really bad happened."

I reluctantly made eye contact with him. "He was shot."

Nate's eyes grew large. "Wow. That's serious!"

"They don't even know who shot him," I said. I immediately regretted the words.

"He's probably associated with some rough characters, I would expect." Nate took a bite of his pita and glanced around the cafeteria.

"You know nothing about him." I crossed my arms over my chest. "He's a good person and didn't deserve this. His *family* didn't deserve this."

"I shouldn't have said that. I didn't mean anything by it. Sorry."

I could tell he was just itching to say something like, "Then he should have avoided that career path," or something equally obnoxious. I know *I* would have in his position.

Nate hugged me and I returned to my office. I thought he might ask me out to dinner or on a real date of some kind, but no. He just left and said, "See you later."

I was giving up a huge piece of my life and I didn't even get an offer for a date. It was a real kick in the metaphorical balls, to be quite honest.

I stood in front of the paper shredder, hating everything and everyone around me. Even Nate was starting to aggravate me.

Maybe he doesn't want to date me, just have sex with me.

I stared at the wall as I fed more documents into the machine. My eye twitched as I thought about the whole situation. It was fucked up.

Two days later, Derek finally returned from vacation and gave me a username and password. I was basically a paper shredding ninja by this time. When I logged in for the first time, Derek got me set up with the support chat application and then left before the weirdness started.

Molly: *Hello, my name is Molly. Thank you for using chat support. How may I help you today?*

Bob: *Hi.*

Molly: *Good morning Bob.*

Bob: *I like your name. I once dated a girl named Molly in high school. She was beautiful.*

What the fuck, Bob?

I showed the chat box to Allie.

"Yeah," she said, looking over her shoulder. "That happens a lot. It's going to get a lot creepier than that, I promise."

Molly: *Thank you. How may I help you today Bob?*

Bob: *What are you wearing?*

I glanced over my shoulder to see if anyone was watching me. I turned my Wi-Fi off and on, disconnecting me from the customer and connecting me with the next person in the queue.

Molly: *Hello, my name is Molly. Thank you for using chat support. How may I help you today?*

Stella: *I stapled the cat.*

Molly: *Sorry, I do not understand what you mean.*

Stella: *I stapled the cat with the stapler. What do I do?*

Molly: *Are they … our brand of staples?*

Stella: *YES. WHAT DO I DO? THE CAT KEEPS MEOWING!!!!!!!!*

Molly: *Take it to a vet?*

Stella: *Are you going to pay for it cause I'm not!!!!*

Molly: *I'm sorry. We cannot be held responsible for you stapling your cat. How did that even happen??*

Stella: *I was scrapbooking and Mrs. Jiffy Pop jumped up on the table and I went right down on her tail. She is still meowing. What should I do????*

I had four "normal" customers with actual questions for the rest of the day. I had three more idiots, two more perverts and a partridge in a pear tree. I browsed Facebook when the queue was clear.

Around three o'clock, Brenda noticed I wasn't doing much so she put me back on shredder duty.

I was almost done shredding documents by quarter after four.

Maybe if I finish this pile, I can go home. Do people just go home when they have finished their work or do they have to wait until five?

My phone buzzed in my pocket. Nobody heard it outside the stock room so I checked the caller ID. It was Audrey.

"Paul woke up," Audrey said. "The doctors expect him to make a full recovery."

I smiled and my eyes filled with tears. "That's good," I squeaked. "Do they know who shot him?"

"No. The shooter was wearing a ski mask and didn't speak before pulling the trigger."

I felt sick, picturing the scene. Poor Paul.

"I also got a call from our friend Rhys today," Audrey added.

"'Friend' might be a strong word."

"I no longer have to employ his friend. He even apologized for that bit." She paused. "He suggested I rehire you instead."

I raised my eyebrows. "He said that?"

"Seems like you've made quite an impression on him."

What the hell does she mean by that?

"Anyway, I'll likely be calling you in a few weeks," she said. "Is that alright?"

Brenda came into the room, a stack of papers in her arms. She flopped them onto the pile I was working through. She glared at me and placed a hand on her hip. I held my index finger up at her—the universal signal for "Wait a moment. I'm on the phone."

"Yes, that's fine," I said to Audrey and hung up.

"You're not supposed to be on the phone during work," Brenda snapped.

"No, it's okay," I said, smiling wide. "I quit."

It's good to be back.

* * *

I'd rather die doing what I love than live doing something I hate.

I repeated this mantra to myself as I walked home from the office building. I hadn't even lasted three full days at my temp job.

I texted Nate, saying I left work early because of a migraine.

Not even three full days? He's going to think/know you're pathetic. Tomorrow. I'll tell him the truth tomorrow.

Yes, he would be disappointed. I would just have to deal with that, and he would just have to deal with me.

I smiled to myself as I unlocked my apartment door. I hummed and moved my shoes to the closet. That's when I saw the back of a head resting on a throw pillow on the couch. Someone was sleeping on my sofa.

Stranger danger!

"Oh my god!" I screamed.

The man turned his head, blinking tired eyes at me. I threw my purse at his head. It landed on the floor beside the couch. My aim was never great.

"You're home early," Rhys said.

CHAPTER FOURTEEN

"This is so posh!" Rhys put his hands on his hips and walked around my apartment, peeking into each room and surveying the contents. "You own this place?"

"I cannot even *believe* you broke into my apartment."

"I'm a thief. It's what I do. And just in case you forgot, it's what you did too until quite recently. Also, I didn't 'break in.' Your neighbor buzzed me in and then let me use her spare key. Charming lady."

Note to self: get spare key back from Mrs. Blumenkrantz. She is useless.

Rhys flopped down on the sofa again, stretching out the full length. He grinned up at me. "Do you have lemonade? Because I'd kill for some lemonade."

"Sorry, I'm fresh out. Also, I'm surprised you didn't just look in the fridge yourself after you *broke in.*" I crossed my arms crossed over my chest. "Why are you here?" I spoke louder this time.

He sat up, looking as giddy as a teenager with a secret to share. "I've got an assignment coming up in the next few days and I'd like you to join me on it."

"No thanks."

"You just got fired from a pathetic office job," he laughed. "You are in no position to turn this down."

Why must he always know so much about me? Ugh!

"Actually, I wasn't fired. I quit."

"Why?" Rhys said. "Wasn't it completely inspiring to feel what a normal person feels in their nine-to-five every day?"

"It didn't agree with me."

"But you're back to your old tricks again, I assume."

"That's none of your business."

"Well, it sort of is, actually. I just want to make sure Audrey called you."

My whole body tensed.

"If you already knew Audrey was rehiring me, then why the fuck did you play dumb?" I wanted to strangle him. "Why do you always have to be so—"

"Charming?"

"Annoying!"

He shrugged. "It's a gift."

"Good for you. Can you leave now?"

He didn't leave the sofa. "Did Audrey offer you any assignments?"

"No," I said, jaw clenched.

"Wonderful. You're free to travel to London with me in a few days then."

"I'm not doing another assignment with you." *Or anyone, for that matter.* "I can't trust you."

My cell buzzed. Rhys eyed my hip where my phone was pocketed.

"Aren't you going to get that?"

"Maybe later."

"You should answer it now. Might be important."

I sighed and took out my phone. It was an email notification concerning a bank transfer of five hundred thousand dollars, sent to me by an anonymous user.

I giggled with glee in my head. *Half a million dollars for meeeeeee! How nice of Rhys to give me back my money.*

I tilted my chin up to look at him. "Alright, Rhys. You have my attention."

"I'm sorry … for what I did … with your money. It was wrong," he said. "Even if you didn't agree to do this assignment with me, you should still have your money. Like everyone in this line of work, I'm unapologetically greedy. I promise never to steal from you again. It was a mistake I completely regret."

I didn't say anything. I didn't know if I should believe a single word coming from his mouth. But he *had* returned my money to me. My opinion of him was slowly improving.

"Have you ever heard of *Kiss Me Once, Kill Me Twice?*"

"No…?"

"It's a James Bond movie they started filming in the mid-sixties. They decided to scrap the footage and started filming *Thunderball* instead. You can see some bits and pieces of what survived on YouTube. It looked promising." He glanced at me. "Please tell me you've seen the James Bond movies."

"I think I saw *Skyfall.*" I shrugged.

"No, I mean the originals. *Dr. No? Goldfinger? From Russia with Love?*" He stared at me. "Sean Connery?"

"I know who he is. I just..." I shrugged again.

"He is a national treasure!" He frowned at me and continued. *"Anyway.* There was a classic Aston Martin designed for the movie before they shut down production. You and I are going to steal that car." He paused. "And probably some jewelry while we're at it."

"What kind of jewelry?"

"Some very large and sparkly rocks, kid. And lots of them."

Inside, I was salivating. That feeling of combined lust and adrenaline was making my thoughts fuzzy.

"Who is the client?"

"Simon Brooks. He's an American. I think he's in oil or something. Loves all things James Bond."

I nodded, urging him to continue.

"We pick up the car at night while the owner is hosting some event thing. Lots of people around and the owners will be occupied. We drive it into a delivery truck located at a farm and then take it to a warehouse, where we exchange cash for a car." Rhys paused. "Or I keep the car."

"Why would you keep the car?"

He strolled to the fridge. "You *did* hear me say 'James Bond car,' right?"

He took out a plastic jug of orange juice and twisted off the cap. He gulped right from the mouth of the container.

"Sure, you can have some orange juice. Make yourself at home. Please take your backwash with you."

"Backwash is just Mother Nature's way of saying, 'You've got too much of your drink in your mouth and you must be rid of it.' It's natural, Molly." He put the lid on and slid the juice back into the fridge.

Guess I gotta go to the grocery store and get more juice later.

"Why do you want me to join you?"

Rhys grinned. "Because you love money almost as much as I do. Two million dollars. One million each, right down the middle."

A million dollars? He should have led with that.

"Uh-huh," I said. "So, why share it with me?"

"Because I need you."

I raised my eyebrows. "Excuse me?"

Rhys sat back down on the sofa and looked directly into my eyes. "It's a pretty big job. I know I'll need backup, and I trust your skills. You have no reason to trust me ... but I need your help. I'll beg if I have to." His expression was completely serious.

He's right. I really have no reason to trust him.

"How do we get into this building?"

Rhys's expression quickly melted away into his usual arrogant smirk. "I found the event planner's files and added a Mr. and Mrs. Duncan to the guest list. Simon has assured me the best way into the building is as guests at the event. We're going to have to pose as American since I assume you can't fake a British accent—"

"Wait, we're actually *going* to the event? Are you serious? We'll be seen, probably photographed. Rhys, I am *not* going to jail for you—"

"We're obviously going to wear costumes." He rolled his eyes.

"Disguises? I'm a thief, not a spy from ... from—"

"A James Bond movie?"

171

"Exactly. No. No way!"

"Remember what I looked like when we met?"

The long hair, the Italian accent and the disgusting rodent beard thing on his chin. How could I forget?

"I remember you looking like a tool."

"Exactly. I know my way around costumes. I mean, look at me now."

"Still a tool."

He narrowed his eyes and surveyed my face. "Gotta get you some colored contact lenses and get rid of those freckles, to start."

"But I like my freckles," I mumbled.

"They're lovely. And distinct. Can't have that. I promise, you will not look like Molly Miranda. Or Betty Bruce, for that matter."

I sat back on the couch and stared at the ceiling.

This whole thing sounds ridiculous and risky. But a million dollars! That's a lot of money.

"And when exactly is this event happening?"

"Six days from now. I'd love to offer you time to think about it but I unfortunately don't have that luxury."

I stood up and stared out the window at the vast and glorious view of the city, thinking about the life I live and risk so often. If it were with any other person, I would have said yes in a second. If it had been a job assigned by Audrey, I'd be hopping on a plane by now and enthusiastic to get going.

If I do this, it'll be the biggest payout I've ever received. It's the big leagues.

My head said, "No. No, no, no." But my heart said, "Let's make some mad cheddar, yo."

"I'll do it."

There was a knock at the front door.

The doorman just let someone up here? Perfect.

I whispered at Rhys. "Don't say a word."

I checked the peephole. It was Nate, holding a bouquet.

Fuck.

I opened the door a few inches and squeezed into the doorway. "Hi, Nate."

He smiled. "Hi. How's your head?"

I raised an eyebrow.

Right. The migraine.

"It's pretty bad. Yeah ... it's pretty bad."

My head started doing this weird, exaggerated nodding thing. I was suddenly a human bobble head.

Way to sound like a liar, idiot.

"That sucks."

I was still nodding. Stupid head momentum.

"Yeah. I think it was the ... fluorescent lights ... and the ... um ... photocopier."

"The photocopier?"

"Yeah. I was working near it. It's really loud."

"That's too bad. You should see if they can move you to another desk."

"Sure."

Nate smiled shyly. "Molly, I want you to know that I appreciate the effort that you're making. I know it's not really your thing but you're trying and that's what matters. If you're feeling better tonight or tomorrow, I'd love to grab dinner and go on an actual date—"

"Hey, Molly, I have go." Rhys flung open the door from

my side and squeezed past me, almost running right into Nate.

I am going to murder that man, I swear to god.

"Oh, sorry about that." Rhys nodded at Nate and strolled down the hall.

Nate turned his head slowly back to me. "A migraine, huh?"

"He's a friend."

It was the simplest lie I could come up with.

"You don't *have* friends," he snapped. "Are you fucking him?"

Oh, no, he didn't!

"Whoa! No. I'm not fucking him. I can barely *stand* the guy!"

"Then why was he in your apartment?"

My brain and my mouth completely disconnected. An average of 6.8 lies formed in my head but none of them would come out of my mouth.

"Forget it." He dropped the flowers and stormed off down the hall to the elevator.

I started after him but the older lady in the apartment across from mine poked her head out.

I smiled weakly at her, slowing to a stop. "Hi, Mrs. Blumenkrantz. How are you?"

"Could you kids stop swearing and yelling and stomping down the hall? I'm trying to watch my stories."

"Sorry, Mrs. Blumenkrantz. We'll be quiet."

She shut her door and I launched into a run, only to see the gold elevator doors at the end of the hall sliding shut. Nate glared at me from between the doors. The reflective metal showed me panting slightly, a look of desperation painted on my face.

I looked helpless. I didn't like looking like that.

CHAPTER FIFTEEN

Six days later, Rhys and I checked into a London hotel under assumed names, posing as American tourists. I made a joke about Big Ben compensating for something. The concierge was not impressed.

I checked my phone again when we got into the room. And then a minute later.

"He's not going to text you back," Rhys said, unzipping his suitcase. "He thinks you cheated on him."

"How could I have cheated on him? We weren't even technically dating."

"Fair enough. Seems a little possessive to me."

"Just protective." I shrugged. "I don't know. I guess it doesn't matter at this point."

I flopped down on the bed and closed my eyes. I hadn't slept on the plane. I'd been having trouble sleeping since the thing with Nate happened. I'd lied to him so many times. He didn't know me. Maybe I didn't actually know him either.

There was a knock at the door. Knock, knock. Knock, knock, knock. Knock.

I raised an eyebrow at Rhys as he opened the door. An androgynous woman in a slick navy blue pinstriped suit carrying a dry-cleaning bag and a suitcase nodded at Rhys and stepped inside. Her short green hair was cut at a sharp angle at the bangs and her eye makeup mimicked David Bowie's in *Labyrinth*.

I sat up on the bed. I hadn't been expecting company. Or aliens.

I stared at Rhys. "Who is this?"

Rhys rolled his eyes. "Calm down. This is Margot and she's a genius."

"Rhys gave me your measurements," she said in a thick accent, something between French and Russian. "I have a dress for you."

I eyed Rhys. "And how exactly do you know my measurements?"

"You do a lot of online shopping." He shrugged.

"I actually brought a dress with me. Just a classic little black dress," I said. "I'm good."

"A little black dress isn't going to cut it for this event. It's black-tie." Rhys pulled his toothbrush from his bag. "I figured you wouldn't have a gown, so I put in an order."

"The dress is fine." I glared at Rhys.

Margot pursed her lips. "But can your little black dress hold climbing gear, a glass cutter, jewels and a gun?"

"I usually just keep my ID in my bra." I glanced at Rhys. "'Cause I'm a classy lady."

Margot hung up the bag and unzipped the side.

My mouth dropped open.

The gown was gorgeous. The top was a strapless, ocean blue, jeweled corset. The full skirt was a mass of big ruffles that looked like deep sea waves.

"Whoa."

"I didn't want to make it too—how you say—flashy but it will do." She lifted up one side of the skirt. "This comes off if you need to run. There is a short skirt with pockets and shorts under that if you need them. The dress is long enough to hide your shoes so you can wear flats with it. Just don't wear sneakers. I have shoes for you. They are very nice."

Margot lifted up the top layer of the skirt to unveil big pockets where I could keep several items. It was kind of amazing.

She dropped the skirt back down and pointed at a discreet pocket at hip level. "And you can put your lipstick in there."

"But feel free to keep your ID between your boobs." Rhys grinned.

"This dress is incredible," I said. "Thank you so much."

"I am getting paid, cupcake. It is not a gift." Margot didn't even look at me as she spoke, continuing to look over the dress and smooth out various creases and puckers in the fabric.

I touched the ruffles, checking the weight of the dress. I looked at Margot. "It's so light. And it doesn't make a swishing sound!"

"I told you. She's a genius." Rhys smiled.

Margot put the suitcase on the bed. "We have a lot of work to do."

She worked like a meticulous sculptor.

My eyebrows were lightened and plucked. ("You do not pluck often, do you?" "No. Do they look that bad?" "Yes.") False eyelashes were applied. My freckles were covered. My eyes went from blue-green to brown. The studs in my ears were replaced with dangling diamonds. ("These are kind of heavy. Do you have any other—" "Stop talking.") My hair was tucked under an elegant wig. Margot worked to make sure every chocolate brown wave and curl was hairsprayed into submission. ("Don't worry about this wig. You will need a chainsaw to get it off.")

"I feel like I'm doing undercover work," I said to Margot. "Like in *Charlie's Angels* or something."

Margot ignored me and kept working on my French manicure. Well, applying French manicured fake nails over my nasty, chewed-up nails. Same difference.

Rhys came out of the bathroom, adjusting a cufflink. Despite the wig, the prosthetic nose, the makeup and how crazy he made me feel 99% of the time, he looked hella dashing.

He caught me looking at him and smiled.

"Wow," I said.

"I know. I'm really sexy."

He ruined the nice moment. Of course.

Margot stood back and admired her handiwork.

"Alright, cupcake. Stand up and—how you say—twirl."

I did as instructed since I was genuinely terrified of her.

I stood in front of the mirror and gaped. "Holy shit."

It was like I was in someone else's body. It was kind of surreal. Plus, my waist looked tiny and my boobs looked magnificent.

This must be how girls feel when they are transformed for their high school prom. Maybe I should have gone to mine.

I could see Rhys staring at my reflection in the mirror. I looked over my shoulder at him.

"What do you think?"

He nodded and broke off eye contact. "You look nice."

Margot handed him a box. He scooped out a diamond necklace. He stepped closer to me, cleared his throat and put the ornate necklace around my neck, fastening it in the back. His knuckles brushed up against my neck as he fumbled with the clasp. He stepped away and cleared his throat again.

"You, uh, missed some freckles on her shoulders."

Margot waved him aside and dusted some more makeup onto my clavicle.

Half an hour later, we took a back exit out of the hotel and got into a black cab.

It was show time.

* * *

We drove up a long driveway, passing a brightly lit lawn dotted with well-groomed topiaries. High shrubs acted as a fence around the whole property, with an old, multi-level stone mansion situated in the middle at the end. The sun was setting, slipping behind the tall chimneys.

If your property looks like this, you obviously have too much money and deserve to get robbed.

"No gate," Rhys whispered into my ear.

The driver's eyes darted to the mirror. I giggled,

pretending Rhys said something witty or sweet—fat chance of that.

The driver opened the door for us. I wasn't used to being in plain sight during an assignment. I felt like I might throw up at any moment.

Oh well. Just aim for Rhys's head or something.

Rhys offered his arm to me and I took it, switching my glittery clutch purse to the other hand.

"You have our tickets, right, darling?" Rhys asked in a perfect American accent.

How the hell does he do that? Whatever. Two can play that game.

"Yes, of course, darling," I said in an English accent.

Rhys smirked and nodded. "Well done," he said, switching to English as well. "Well done indeed." His accent was better than mine. He sounded like Audrey— British and well financed from birth.

At the front door we joined the queue. Every other couple nearby seemed to have the same accent as Rhys. All of the men were in tuxes while women wore glamorous gowns of all shapes and colors. They all seemed to know one another—all members of some old money club where tennis, equestrian, sailing and high tea with the duchess were just part of daily life. I listened to tidbits of conversations around me.

"I hope Stella isn't wearing the same gown as I am. It was *such* an embarrassment the last time."

"Did I tell you my son drove our boat into the dock last week? *What* a disaster."

"Oh dear. I suppose he's off to rehab again?"

Rhys nudged me gently, looking at the far left of the

wide building before us. Beside the end of the building was a detached, newer building—a garage.

We moved up in line and handed our tickets to a man with a list. He peered at us over his tiny round glasses.

"John and Beth Duncan," he said, looking for our names on the list and flipping to the next page.

I glanced at Rhys and smiled back at the man.

Where are our names? Rhys, you said you took care of this. I feel sick. I think my underwear is creeping up. I hope my upper lip isn't sweating. What if my wig falls off? Oh my fuck, where the fuck are our fucking names?

"Ah, yes. Mr. and Mrs. Duncan, right this way."

We smiled. I tried not to heave a sigh of relief, as that would seem suspicious. We followed another man into a grand lobby that led to a ballroom.

A sign, positioned on an easel, stood by the door, reading the event name in fancy calligraphy: *The Fox-Hartford Foundation for Women Benefit*. Rhys saw it and his cheeks went pale. Audrey's charity.

I'm going to be sick.

CHAPTER SIXTEEN

Rhys stuffed shrimp into his mouth and tried to appear calm. Trying to be invisible in the middle of a crowded ballroom is hard.

"What do we do?" I said. "Audrey will murder us if she sees us."

"She might not recognize us."

"We should leave. I'm not stealing from Audrey—"

"This isn't her house," he said, smiling and nodding at an older gentleman who smiled at him first. "Audrey has a house in London. This place belongs to a friend of hers. An heiress who spends all her time doing charity stuff."

"So you know this lady's life story," I said through a clenched jaw. "Yet you didn't realize the event we were going to was for Audrey's charity?"

Rhys grimaced. "The event wasn't under the charity's name. So, no. I didn't see that. What are the chances—"

I put up my a hand. "I got it. Brilliant work, as always.

We should go—"

Rhys grabbed a flute of champagne from a waiter passing by and basically shoved it into my hand. "We're doing this. Relax."

I sipped at the champagne while glaring at my partner in crime. I wanted to down my drink in one swig but didn't because gulping champagne makes me farty.

I bet the people at this event don't even fart. Especially that woman over there.

That particular woman seemed to attract a lot of attention, especially from the men. Her wavy blond hair gleamed like gold as she mingled. Her gown flattered her hourglass frame and flaunted her boobs with a daring V-shaped slit down the front.

Rhys saw where I was looking and glanced over. "Oh, wow."

"What, who is that?"

"I can't even believe it. That's Ivy Dixon."

"The woman from the painting we stole?"

"Yup." He gave her another once-over, his eyes lingering inappropriately long. "Oh, yeah. That's definitely her."

He kept staring at her.

"Darling, if you're going to play my husband tonight, perhaps you could not ogle the supermodel."

"But doesn't that make it more realistic?"

"I know how much you care about being in character. But seriously. Knock it off."

"Think I could get off with her if we weren't here for a job?"

"Not a chance. Let's get out of here. You'll just have to tell your client that we can't—"

"I will do no such thing." Rhys jerked his head down to look at me. "We're sticking to the plan. Even if Audrey sees us, there's nothing she can do."

"You two must be Beth and John Duncan."

We both looked over out shoulder. Audrey sipped on a flute of champagne, smiling.

Busted.

Perhaps she just *sensed* people were talking about her and flew in like a frickin' vampire to investigate.

"I am so glad you could join us for this little fundraiser."

Is there actually a chance she doesn't recognize us?

I swallowed and didn't speak. I glanced at Rhys.

"Yes, well…" He cleared his throat. "Anything to help a good cause."

She lowered her voice as she spoke but maintained the ultra-polite tone I wasn't used to. "Perhaps you two can have a bite to eat, a few drinks and then be on your way."

Ah. She knows it's us.

"But this is the event of the season." Rhys squared his shoulders. "We'd hate to miss out on all the fun."

"There will be *no fun*," Audrey snapped, teeth clenched. "Please don't make me call security."

"Wouldn't that just cause suspicion among the other guests?" I asked. "By the way, that's a lovely necklace. Wherever did you get it?"

Rhys glanced at me but I never broke eye contact with Audrey.

The necklace Dad and I had found in the tunnel in Key West was draped around her neck. It had been cleaned up real nice since the last time I saw it, but it was definitely the same one.

Dad didn't fence that necklace for me. He gave it to his awful girlfriend. Well, that's just great.

Audrey sighed and sipped her drink again. "I don't know what the two of you are doing here but I suggest that you change your minds and move along—"

"Audrey, darling!" Ivy Dixon appeared at Audrey's side. "You just disappeared! I wanted to introduce you to..." Her gaze wandered over to Rhys. "Oh, hello. I don't believe we've met." Her voice was soft and breathy, like Jessica Rabbit.

"John Duncan." Rhys took her hand and kissed the top of it. "It's a pleasure to meet you, Miss Dixon."

She giggled, flashing a perfect smile. Her piercing green eyes looked right past me. Audrey and I exchanged disgusted looks.

Audrey smiled weakly. "This is his wife, Julia."

"Beth."

"Whatever." Audrey took another sip.

Drink up, Audrey. I'd love to see you get hammered and look like an idiot this evening. In fact, it would really make this whole thing worth it.

"So, what kind of business are you in, John Duncan?"

"I'm an archeologist," he said without a hint of hesitation.

Audrey rolled her eyes and glared at the ceiling.

"That sounds fascinating," Ivy said, touching his arm. "I'd love to hear all about it. We should have dinner sometime so we can talk a bit more. I adore astrology."

"Archeology," I corrected.

Ivy didn't even glance at me. "Whatever."

"Ivy, darling, there are so many people here anxious to meet you. I think you're the reason most people bought tickets to this event," Audrey said with a laugh.

Ivy tapped Rhys on the tip of the nose with her manicured finger and smiled. "We must talk more later tonight, John Duncan." She followed Audrey and winked at Rhys before disappearing into the crowd.

He looked back at me. "What? Why are you glaring at me?"

"We're supposed to be married."

"But we're not. We're pretending," he whispered, glancing around.

I finished off my champagne. "We're here to do a job. We're not here to get laid."

Rhys grinned. "You're jealous."

"I'm not jealous," I said, my voice slipping out of the English accent for a second. "I just want to do this thing *right*. Do you understand?"

"Alright, Mrs. Duncan." He took my hand and kissed it. "I am sorry. Let me get you another drink."

An hour went by and people were getting drunk quicker than I expected. Several couples left their complimentary shrimp in exchange for the dance floor. Seeing this, the DJ put on some slow music.

"Let's dance," Rhys whispered.

I shook my head. "I'd rather not have a lot of attention on us. Audrey already—"

He grabbed my hand and led me to the dance floor. He pulled me close, his left hand sliding down to the small of my back. He smiled and took my hand in his right.

"Some people were looking at us *because* we weren't dancing," he whispered directly into my ear, his warm breath tickling my neck. "Just follow my lead."

When I was preparing to be a professional thief, knowing how to dance was close to the bottom of my to-do list, so I was thankful Rhys seemed to know what he was doing.

Also, he smelled nice.

Rhys rested his cheek against my forehead as we swayed. The song changed a few times but we stayed in place. More couples joined the floor and the champagne kept flowing.

I could see Audrey in the corner talking to a man. She glanced over at us occasionally but she was mostly just trying to keep her distance. Ivy was slow dancing with a man who looked about ninety—probably the richest guy she could find.

Rhys kissed my forehead and I looked up at him, alarmed.

"Don't take this the wrong way," he whispered, "but I'm going to kiss you now."

Before I could say anything, Rhys put his hands on my face—like they do in the movies—and brought his lips to mine. It was passionate, intense and made me kind of tingly. My fingers somehow found the back of his neck while his arms were wrapped tightly around my waist.

I suppose when you have as much practice kissing women as Rhys does, you get good at it. Despite knowing it was all just for show, my heart was pounding and my face was hot.

He pulled his mouth from mine and cleared this throat.

"We should go home now," he said, glancing around at a few couples who were staring at us.

I nodded dumbly up at him. "Okay."

He took my hand and led me from the ballroom. I glanced over my shoulder to see Audrey slow dancing with the man from earlier and not paying attention to us.

Rhys stopped in the empty lobby and took out his phone. He showed me the screen. Then he just switched off all the security cameras in the building with the press of a button.

Oh, yes. We're here to steal the car. I thought we were going to … never mind.

"Are you ready to do this?"

I nodded and followed him up the stairs.

CHAPTER SEVENTEEN

The rest of the estate was deserted, so we could easily move between rooms as long as we stayed away from the lobby and ballroom. The place was a maze of bedrooms, sitting rooms and squeaky-clean bathrooms. We found a home theater, a spa and a private art gallery.

"We could take one." Rhys pointed to a small painting that looked like it was from Holland. "It's tiny and you have a dozen pockets in that gown."

I adjusted one of my gloves. "Don't get distracted."

We made our way from room to room. We were in a hallway when I grabbed Rhys's arm and pulled him into a bedroom closet.

"Molly, we don't have time for a shag right now."

"Shut up," I hissed into the darkness, slapping my hand over his mouth. "Someone's coming."

The sound of footsteps got louder and closer. The steps were heavy, probably from flat shoes and not heels. I put my other hand over my mouth to muffle the sound of my breathing. We froze in place. The person stopped at the doorway and slowly walked into the room. They were three feet from us, just a closet door between us and them.

"Harold!" someone shouted from the hall. "We're out of ice downstairs."

Harold left the room in a rush, closing the door behind him. We waited a few minutes before silently slipping out of the closet. I surveyed the room.

It was a grand bedroom with an enormous, ornate canopy bed. A ton of lush burgundy fabric hung from the ceiling. The walls were deep red, with gold trim. Everything in the room looked antique, with a romantic ambience. This had to be the master bedroom.

A long mahogany chest of drawers lined the back wall with a vanity mirror and a chair at the end. Rhys went for the nearby jewelry box. He pocketed a string of pearls, diamond earrings and a gold watch. He riffled through the drawers and found some more glittery things, but no car keys.

"My client said the car keys would be in the master bedroom," Rhys said, sliding the last drawer shut. "They have to be here somewhere."

I looked around the room some more and happened to glance back into the closet we'd been hiding in. Sitting on the floor, right next to where we'd been standing, was a safe about two feet high. It was an older model with a combination dial, popular in these big old homes.

I pawed through my layers of gown and found my stethoscope in a pocket. Rhys looked at me over his shoulder.

I put my stethoscope around my neck with the earpieces

in my ears and the chest piece pressed up against the front of the safe, close to the dial. Rhys stood watch at the door so I could work in silence.

I pressed my fingers against the cold metal door to feel the clicking motions inside as I turned the dial. I turned the knob slowly the other way until I heard another click. "Sixty-five, eleven and…" I turned it slowly back the other way, listening hard. Almost there. "Twenty-one."

I spun the handle and the door popped open. I looked up at Rhys. He grinned.

"What?"

"I've never seen anyone in an evening gown crack a safe before. It's kind of sexy."

Inside the safe were bundles of British cash. At the back of the safe was a hook. I reached back into the dark safe and pulled the keychain hanging from it. It was a leather tag decorated with an Aston Martin logo, an old car key dangling from it.

Bingo.

Rhys found a window we could fit through and checked out our escape route. Now that we had the key, it was probably much safer to exit that way. The party would be wrapping up soon. We had to get a move on before guests started pouring out into the courtyard.

The bedroom door opened. A security guy poked his head in and stared at me.

"What are you doing?" he barked, reaching out to grab my arm.

"Molly!" Rhys yelled from the window.

I rolled my eyes and slipped my hand into a pocket of

my gown. I grabbed the syringe inside, uncapped it with my thumb and jammed the needle into the security guy's arm. His eyes rolled back in his head and he fell to the floor.

Rhys grabbed his hands and dragged him further inside, closing the door behind him.

"Why did you yell my name?" I shook my head at him. "That was dumb."

"I was concerned! When the hell did you steal one of my syringes?"

"When we were dancing." I smiled.

"Clever girl."

"I won't be able to climb down a roof with this dress." I stepped over the security guy's sleeping body. "Help me get the skirt off."

"Just the skirt?" He smirked.

"Yes," I snapped. "And I'm wearing your jacket out of here."

He sighed. "Fine."

I sat on the edge of the bed and Rhys helped me unsnap and unzip the skirt from where it was attached to the shorter skirt underneath, the one with all the pockets. I slipped on his jacket and tossed the bundled-up skirt under the bed.

We climbed out of the windows and onto the flat roof, making sure to stay low until we could find a place to climb down. From this end of the manor, we could see the roof of the garage. At the side of the garage was a door. Between the manor and the garage was an enormous oak tree with long overhanging branches. If we could get to the tree, we could climb over to the garage roof.

If only it were that simple. Located behind the garage and the manor was a grand garden with topiaries, a fountain and everything. A couple had strayed into the garden to get some fresh air and privacy. If either of them looked up, they would see us climbing the tree.

"Shit," Rhys whispered, rolling up his shirtsleeves to his elbows.

I removed the rest of my skirt and left all the other items that were in the pockets on the roof. I wouldn't be able to climb with them. The only thing I took was the Aston Martin key and my cell phone from my clutch. I stuffed them both down the front of my corset.

Rhys raised his eyebrows. "You know, I can carry something if you need me to."

I readjusted the key so it wasn't poking me in the side boob. "Nah. I'm good."

I felt pretty damn naked, though, only wearing a corset, Lycra shorts, loafers and a suit jacket that was too big for me. And it was getting cold.

Rhys stayed low to the ground and pulled himself up onto an overhanging branch. I followed. The branches were thick so the tree didn't move as we held on to them.

The bark scratched my bare legs as I held on to a branch over my head. I moved my feet around, trying to get my balance but there weren't any branches close enough. My fingers were in agony as I held onto a branch. The loafers weren't offering much of a grip either.

"Um," I whispered over to him, "I need help here."

Some bark fell from the branch and I dangled by one arm.

"Molly! Hang on!"

"Would you *please* stop yelling my goddamn name!" I hissed.

Rhys grabbed my arm and pulled me to a thicker branch, and I held onto the tree trunk and let my sore fingers rest.

"We have to go," he whispered. "Now."

He grabbed a branch and moved towards the garage, but the branch gave way under his weight and he fell with a loud, hard thud.

"Oh my god!" one of the people in the garden shouted. "Are you alright?"

Without thinking, I jumped out of the tree and landed on my feet. I stumbled backwards and fell on my ass—on purpose.

"He's okay. He didn't even feel it!" I yelled back. "This is a great party, eh?"

I was trying to sound as drunk as possible, while still using my British accent. Thankfully, my British accent sounds a bit drunk anyway.

I stayed low in the grass and hid half of myself behind the tree. They might be suspicious of someone in shorts. Drunk, rich people climb trees all the time, right?

"Are you okay?" I whispered to Rhys. The grass was cold and soft beneath me.

"I think." He winced and rubbed his wrist.

"Oh my goodness!" the other half of the couple said.

They were rushing over to see if we were okay. I had to stop them from getting too close.

I'm going to regret this, I just know it.

On my hands and knees, I wrapped my arms around Rhys's neck and made out with him rather aggressively— basically his entire face. I needed to be gross.

194

The couple stopped dead in their tracks. "Oh dear!"

They rushed into the manor instead, seeing as we were all right, just intoxicated and handsy.

"Get your hands off my ass." I stood up, wiggled my corset top up further and headed for the garage. "Let's go."

Rhys got to his feet and grinned. "You just couldn't wait to kiss me again, could you?" He dusted off his knees.

"Yes. That branch breaking was in my plan all along."

Rhys knelt by the door to the garage a few feet away and retrieved his lock pick from his pocket. "We better hurry," he said. "We don't have much time."

While he was still peering into the lock, I reached over and turned the door handle. It opened with a creak. He glared up at me. I smiled wide.

Once inside, we locked the door behind us and didn't turn on any lights. I used the light from my phone to find the garage door opener switch. Inside the unusually tidy garage was a red convertible with leather seats. Although I couldn't see well, I knew exactly what was parked beside it.

A blue-gray 1964 two-door Aston Martin DB5, gleaming like it was right out of the factory. Rhys caressed its curves like it was a lady.

"Oh, Molly." He sighed. "Can I keep it?"

"Yeah. I don't think so. Start it up." I tossed him the key.

He opened the door like it was made of glass, slowly sliding into the driver's seat so he could enjoy every moment. Gently shutting the door, he caressed the contour of the steering wheel. He slid the key in and smiled as the car purred to life.

I hit the button to open the garage. I slid into the

passenger seat and Rhys slammed on the gas as soon as the garage door was high enough to escape from.

People in front of the building shouted as we sped past them. I heard one of them yell something about the car but I couldn't make out the rest.

We zipped down the driveway and then down the country road. Rhys was laughing with exhilaration as we flew around corners and swerved around other cars.

"We did it," he yelled. "We fucking did it!"

I squealed and slapped my hands on the dash. "Oh my god, I can't believe it—"

"Don't slap the James Bond car. You don't do that."

I slumped down in my seat. "Where's this truck we're supposed to meet up with?"

"I think it's down here." Rhys's eyes narrowed as he approached a dirt road and slowed to turn.

We drove past acres of farmland in the dark. My heart was racing. We finally found the old stone farmhouse where we were to meet Simon.

Rhys checked the map on his phone. "This is it." He turned the car into the driveway. A delivery truck was parked in an old dilapidated barn, a metal ramp set up for us leading into the truck.

We slowly drove up the ramp into the back of the empty truck until the car was completely hidden. He shut off the car, taking the key from the ignition. It was dark in the car, the only light from a dim bulb in the barn. I turned on my phone's flashlight app.

"Now what?"

Rhys took off his wig, his hair sweaty and matted

underneath. "Now you and I are going to go meet Simon inside."

The doors of the delivery truck clanged shut behind us. Now it was completely dark inside.

"Rhys, what's going on?"

The truck was only wide enough to open the car doors a few inches and squeeze out but we managed to get out of the vehicle. I looked into the pitch black around us. Even with the light from my phone I couldn't see anything except for a tiny red light mounted on the truck ceiling. It started to blink and beep before spewing thick gray fog down on us from a tiny spout. Rhys coughed and grabbed on to the open car door as his knees gave way. He slumped against the side of the car. There was a smacking sound as his forehead hit the floor.

"Oh my god, Rhys," I squeaked as I sank to the floor, coughing and gasping for breath in the darkness.

CHAPTER EIGHTEEN

My head was pounding when I woke up. Everything was blurry.

I fought to stay awake. My wrists were tied together behind my back, probably with duct tape. My ankles were bound too. My shoulders ached. I couldn't hear anything, only silence and the quiet scuffling of my body wriggling against a cement floor as I tried to sit up. My gasps were short and fast and my heart thundered.

My vision cleared just enough to look around. I was in a warehouse with a high ceiling and a dusty, cold floor. My wig and prosthetic nose were gone. Rhys was tied up next to me.

With what little energy I had, I wiggled closer to him and nudged his leg with my toes.

"Rhys," I whispered. "Rhys, wake up."

He moaned quietly and slowly opened his eyes. He looked at my face, his cheek flat against the floor.

"Where are we?"

"I don't know."

He tried to wriggle out of his wrist restraints, his neck turning red as he pulled. The restraints didn't budge. We both looked around the warehouse. The industrial lights overhead were bright, the one on the end flickering. There were no windows, just a wide door at the end with a small square office beside it.

In the middle of the warehouse was a small table. Standing proudly in the middle of the table was the Egyptian fertility artifact from Oklahoma. (Ya know, the one with the boner.)

Oh my god. The gunman. He's going to finish the job. This is where I'm going to die. Right here in this warehouse.

"We have to get out of here now," I whispered.

Rhys rolled over to face away from me. "Do you think you could get the tape from around my wrists?"

I shuffled over and felt around the silver tape to find an edge I could rip off, my bound hands making it almost impossible to move. The tape was wrapped around his wrists several times. I found an edge and peeled it away, causing a loud ripping to echo through the empty warehouse.

The door to the office flew open and a woman walked toward us. She was tall and thin and had short, dark hair, long legs and a gun.

"I wouldn't do that if I were you," she shouted from across the warehouse floor, aiming her gun at us.

Rhys's eyes narrowed. "Casey?"

Rhys's off-and-on partner kidnapped us? That doesn't make any sense.

I looked back at the woman—now close enough for me

to see her face.

This is just unbelievable.

I gaped up at her. "Tegan?"

This is what happens when a woman hits on me. She ends up being a psychopath.

Rhys stared at me. "Who the fuck is Tegan?"

"Actually, my name is Lisa," she said, looking down at me. "It's nice that you recognized me this time, though."

I winced, my restraints digging in. "What are you talking about?"

Lisa/Tegan/Casey laughed and rolled her eyes. "We worked together. Remember?"

I stared at her. It took me a few seconds but I figured it out—and she was right.

Lisa/Tegan/Casey was the one Paul partnered me up with years ago. She was that ditzy, disrespectful, useless eighteen-year-old with the ringing cell phone who made me hate working with a partner in the first place. She'd cut her hair short, spoke differently and wore heavy black eyeliner now. That useless eighteen-year-old was long gone.

"You've grown into a lovely young woman," I mumbled.

Lisa kicked me hard in the side and I yelped. I doubled over, as much as a person can with their hands and feet bound.

Yeah, that's gonna bruise.

"Leave her alone," Rhys said in a low voice.

Lisa put her boot firmly on the side of Rhys's face. "Say another word, I dare you," she said.

I frowned and closed my eyes. "So Simon Brooks isn't a real person."

Lisa burst out laughing. "Voice actor." She smiled at

me. "By the way, I'm straight. Just figured you might be a dyke since you're friends with Ruby. She will make friends with *anyone*. Shit, that girl is way too trusting." She laughed loudly and nodded at Rhys. "So is he, by the way."

Rhys looked at me from across the floor, tears in his eyes. He looked terrified but probably no more than I was.

"This bitch got me fired," Lisa said. "After that, nobody wanted to hire me. I had to start over. You fucking ruined me, you *and* Paul."

I glared at her, my throat tightening. "You shot Paul, didn't you?"

Lisa just smiled. "Only a little."

"And you followed me to Oklahoma."

Her smile faded. "I was so pissed when I didn't kill you that night. *So* pissed! Could *not* believe it when my gun jammed. My therapist says I have anger issues. So I decided to pay Paul a visit instead." She walked over to the table and picked up the wooden statue. "This little guy is hilarious. Just decided to keep it for myself."

"You didn't have to kill that guy in Oklahoma."

"He could have seen your face. I don't want you in prison, sweetie." She put the statue back in the middle of the table. "I'm going to kill you for real this time."

"Your career is going really well," Rhys said. "So why are you doing this?"

Lisa knelt down beside Rhys and leaned in close. "You're really handy to have around, Rhys—you and your little gadgets. But you won't work with me anymore." She stood up and spun her pistol on her finger like Annie Oakley.

Rhys swallowed and looked at the floor.

201

"Why don't you tell Molly what you told me?" Lisa whispered.

He exhaled and avoided eye contact. "I told her I didn't want to work with her anymore, just you."

I blinked at him. "Why?"

Lisa rolled her eyes. "Exactly how fucking stupid *are* you, anyway? He's obviously in love with you." She stuck her finger in her mouth and pretended to gag.

Oh.

"Thanks," Rhys mumbled. He looked embarrassed. Ashamed, even.

Lisa swung her leg back and booted Rhys in the knee. He howled in agony, his face contorted, his jaw clenched.

"I can't have my competition running around with his little gadgets, so I'm just going to kill you," Lisa said, looking straight down at Rhys. "But first I'm going to kill your little girlfriend right in front of you, because she's a pain in the ass."

A cell phone rang in Lisa's pocket. "I have to take this. Don't go anywhere."

The tall heels of her boots clicked as she walked back to the office and closed the door behind her.

"Molly," Rhys whispered. "She doesn't know what she's talking—"

"Rhys. Shut up. Roll over."

I worked at the tape a bit more.

"I'm sorry I got you into this—"

"Rhys. Seriously. Stop talking."

"Wait," Rhys said, moving his butt closer to me instead of his hands. "The car key is still in my pocket!"

I had to spoon him to be able to reach into his pocket but I managed to grip the leather tag and pull it out. I held onto the tag and used a sharp edge of the Aston Martin logo to cut through the tape about halfway down.

The office door opened as Rhys tried to separate his wrists behind his back, but the tape would not rip apart. I grabbed the key and held it between my hands, still tied tight together.

"Change of plans!" Lisa shouted. "We're going for a little drive."

CHAPTER NINETEEN

"You two are going to go get into the car in the truck." Lisa pointed to the Aston Martin.

"How are we supposed to do that? Our feet are taped together," Rhys snapped.

Lisa pointed the gun at my head. "Perhaps you should hop like a bunny."

Making tiny, deliberate hops, we made it across the cement floor to the car and Lisa shoved us into the front seats.

She surveyed the car. "Where are the keys?"

"Up your arse," Rhys said, sounding more Scottish than usual.

She cuffed the back of his head and patted him down. She checked above the mirror. A little spare key fell out onto the seat. I looked the other way, hiding my surprise. Lisa snatched up the key.

She shut the doors of the truck behind us, dropping us into darkness. Soon we heard the truck start and felt it move. It was impossible to tell where we were or where we were heading.

"Twist around in your seat so I can get the rest of the tape off your wrists," I said.

This time I chewed my way through the tape since my hands were still grasping tight to the key with the leather tag.

"You're drooling all over my hands."

"Yeah, well, deal with it. I'm probably going to die of glue poisoning."

The tape snapped and his hands were freed. He ripped through the tape on my hands, the tape on my feet and then the tape on his ankles.

Rhys sat back in the plush leather set and sighed. "Now what do we do?"

I smiled coyly and dangled the key from my finger.

"Oh my god!" Rhys grabbed my face and kissed me hard on the mouth. "Sorry. I really need to stop doing that." He snatched the key from me. "We need to switch places."

"I can drive."

"Sure you can."

"No, really. I can drive this car."

Rhys crossed his arms over his chest, one eyebrow arched. He didn't believe me.

"Doesn't mean I *should* drive it, though," I said. "You, either. Every cop in England is going to be on the lookout for this car. If what you tell me is true, it's worth more than the crown jewels."

Rhys shrugged. "Basically."

"And I am *not* going to survive this only to get arrested for theft. That is not happening. Do you understand me?"

"Yes, ma'am."

I sat back in my seat and closed my eyes. I took a deep breath, exhaling slowly.

What would my father do?

* * *

After an hour of driving, the truck stopped. I put the key in the ignition and readied to start the engine. There was some metal clanking sounds at the doors. They opened and I turned the key.

It all happened so fast.

The tires screeched to life as we went flying out of the back of the truck, the back of the car scraping against the doors. We soared backwards through the air, landing with a hard crunch several feet away from the truck.

If this car doesn't move after that little trick, I am going to be so pissed and never watch a James Bond movie ever again!

The car roared to life as I floored it again and tore out of what looked like a different warehouse, this one dimly lit and smaller. A handful of people jumped out of our way. Their faces were blurs as we sped by.

"Oh, fuck!" Rhys shouted. "We hit someone!"

"Are they dead?" I looked around.

"No, I think you just clipped them—"

"Then I don't fucking care!" I changed gears and swerved out of the building and onto a country road.

"Be careful with this car!" Rhys shouted. "I've decided I'd like to keep it after all!"

I didn't know where we were going. I just drove as fast

as I could. It was late at night so road signs and landmarks were invisible. We were in the middle of nowhere. I could make out green fields in the distance, probably farmland.

"We can't stay in this car for very long," I said. "We have to get our bearings and find a place to ditch it." I plucked my phone from my corset top and tossed it to Rhys.

"One bar," he said. "Looks like Audrey tried calling you a couple times."

I passed a slow-moving car on the road as specks of rain hit the windshield. "Audrey will have to wait."

"You're a better driver better than I expected."

"Thanks." I checked the rear-view mirror. "But not fast enough."

Rhys turned around in his seat. The delivery truck was speeding up behind us, getting so close I could see the driver's face—Lisa. She looked furious. She held a gun in one hand and steered with the other.

Rhys stared through the back windshield. "How the hell did she catch up to us when we're in a fucking James Bond car?"

"Maybe the car isn't fast enough—"

"Or maybe it's the driver!" He slammed his foot onto mine to press harder on the gas, jolting the car forward.

"I'd rather not die tonight!" I screamed.

"Me neither! Drive faster!" He sat back in his seat and watched the truck in the mirror. "Blaming the James Bond car," he mumbled. "You've got some nerve."

The rain poured down harder, making it difficult to see where I was driving. I saw a street sign and cranked the wheel, making a sharp left turn.

Kids, if you ever get a chance to drive a luxury vehicle on unfamiliar roads, on the opposite side of the road, in the rain and way over the speed limit … just don't.

Gunfire rang through the air. I checked the mirror. Lisa leaned out of the side of the truck, firing at us. I swerved the car left and right to make us a difficult target. A bullet hit the driver's side mirror, sending it flying off, spinning and hitting the pavement behind us.

The road twisted and turned. Farmland suddenly switched to a rocky coastline. Despite the zigzagging roads, the truck was closer to us but Lisa seemed to be out of bullets for now. I checked my mirror. She was struggling to reload while driving. Somehow the truck picked up speed and bumped the back of our car, jolting us in our seats.

Rhys shook his fist back at her. "The fuck are you doing? You don't intentionally hit the back of a James Bond car!"

I cranked the wheel and made a tight corner. The sound of gunfire rang in my ears. And then the sound of glass shattering. I looked in the rear-view. Tiny shards of glass from the rear window bounced down over the back seat.

"Stop doing that!" he yelled at Lisa.

More shots from the truck. A bullet hit a tire and the car swerved out of control. Bits of shredded rubber flew off the tire. A second bullet flew between Rhys and me, hitting the windshield, causing it to splinter into a million cracks.

"Oh my god! I can't see!" I screamed, gripping the wheel as the car totally ignored where I tried to steer it.

Rhys grabbed the wheel and we veered off into the shallow ditch on the side of the road. Between the rocky cliff on the other side and a grassy ditch, it was probably the better option. The car was resting in the ditch on an angle and I tipped from the driver's seat and fell roughly against Rhys.

The truck's brakes screeched as Lisa tried to navigate the sharp bend in the road. Another car sped around the corner toward her, high beams on. The lights from the truck and the car together were almost blinding. The car swerved left, just in time, to avoid the truck and veered into the ditch, hitting the Aston Martin head-on. Hard. Shattered glass flew at us. Metal crunched around us. Rhys covered my head with his arms, holding me tight.

Before the shattered glass flew at us, I watched the truck, in its own attempt to avoid the car, swerve too far to the right, disappearing over the side of the cliff on the other side of the road.

Everything was silent, except for the tapping of rain on broken glass and twisted metal and the distant sound of waves crashing onto rocks.

Sore but safe, I climbed out of the driver's side door, grabbing my phone from the floor and Rhys's coat from the back seat. Rhys followed me since he couldn't get his door open.

Rhys ran over to the driver in the other car, who was knocked out. Rhys stuck his hand through the broken window and checked his pulse.

"He's alive," he said. "Doesn't seem to have any major injuries."

I frowned at Rhys. "Are you alright—oh my god, you've got a chunk of glass in your arm."

Dazed, Rhys looked down at his arm. "Oh." He looked back at me. "I'm bleeding."

I nodded. "Yeah." I looked around. "More cars will be passing by at any time. We have to get off the road."

We stumbled to the edge of the pavement and looked over the cliff edge. The delivery truck was destroyed, mangled on the jagged rocks below. Angry waves crashed up against the side of the van.

We ran into the woods. Rhys's shirtsleeve was soaked red and he stumbled as he lost more and more blood. I held his arm and kept him running for as long as he could. When he slowed down we stopped and threw ourselves into a soft, wet moss heap under a tree.

"We need to get the glass out of your arm."

Rhys's eyes bulged. "Why-why-why-why do we need to do that? We don't need to do that. Why do we—"

"Because I've watched a lot of movies, and when someone has something in their arm, it always has to get pulled out."

I found a stick and stuck it in his mouth to bite down on. And yes, I saw that in a movie, too. I held the piece of glass carefully between my finger and thumb. "Are you ready? I'm going to count to three. One. Two."

I pulled it out on two. Thankfully, it came out easily and clean. Rhys screamed into the stick and it crunched under his teeth. His face went pale as he stared down at the bloody slice.

I ripped off his other sleeve and tied the fabric around the wound to slow the bleeding. Rhys's lip quivered and he winced in pain.

The bleeding eventually stopped but the rain just kept pouring through the leafy canopy above us. I found some low-hanging branches with thick leaves and spread them out over us as we lay on the cold, damp ground and fell asleep, cuddled together and shivering in the rain.

* * *

"Oh, yeah. I see how it is."

My tired eyes slowly opened. The rain had stopped and sun was shining down in streams between the branches. Rhys was snoring, his arm draped over me and his hand cupping my left boob. I pushed his hand away and looked up at the figure looming over us. I wiped my eyes, just to make sure it was a person and not a ghost.

"Dad?"

He crossed his arms and frowned. "I don't even want to know."

Rhys snorted and sat up. He grabbed his arm and rubbed it. "Oh, shit. Ow."

"Rhys, I believe you've met my father."

He looked up at Dad, saw how close he'd been lying next to me just then and scooted over a bit.

"Good morning," Rhys said, squinting into the sun. "Fine weather we're having, huh? We got lost while camping and—"

Dad held up his hand. "Stop talking, please. We need to get you guys out of here."

On the ride back to civilization, Dad explained what he'd heard from the police scanner overnight and the news early that morning. The driver of the other car woke up shortly after the crash and called an ambulance. An unidentified body was found in the truck over the cliff.

"And the police assume the two thieves who stole the car fled the scene and they are currently on the run," he said. "You may want to lay low for a while."

"Tell me, dear father. Why are you in England?"

"Audrey invited me to her event. The last thing I expected to see when I was there was you two, necking on the dance floor," he said. "I knew something had to be up, especially with those disguises."

I looked at Rhys over my shoulder, resting quietly in the back seat.

"We have to get him to a doctor. I pulled glass out of his arm last night," I said. "How did you find us? How did you know we'd go into the forest?"

"Remember when you were a little girl and I used to take you fishing?"

I nodded.

"Half the time, you weren't really interested. You just wanted to explore the woods. You told me once you felt safe there." He shrugged. "It was the best place to go in this situation. Although I don't recommend crashing an Aston Martin again. You two are lucky to be alive."

I nodded. "I know."

"But even this won't stop you from doing what you do, will it?"

"Probably not."

* * *

The next day, Rhys and I got coffee at Heathrow Airport while waiting for our separate flights. Beneath his black suit jacket his arm was bandaged up and he was on more painkillers than most doctors would usually recommend.

I bought a newspaper to read on the airplane. A big color photo of the James Bond car wreckage had made the front page. Yellow tape and police officers surrounded it.

Rhys whimpered when he saw the photo and read the headline.

"James Bond car stolen and destroyed." He skimmed the article. "The car thieves are on the run... The owners are offering a reward for more information. Hopefully Audrey won't tip them off for the cash."

I sipped my coffee, savoring the sweet brew. "I got a call from Audrey this morning. She is ... well, let's just say she's not happy with either of us."

"Naturally."

"But with Tegan out of the picture—"

"Lisa," Rhys corrected.

"Right. Lisa. Anyway, Audrey is down an agent. She said something about good help being hard to come by." I rolled my eyes. "We may be in the doghouse for a while but I think it'll be okay."

"Did you notice how Lisa took us somewhere else after she got that phone call? What do you think that was about?"

I shook my head. "She may have been working with a contractor. We may never know."

Rhys sighed and stared off into space. I assumed it was the ample amount of morphine in his system putting him to sleep.

"Are you alright?"

He stared down at the table, frowning. "It's just … I'm really upset."

"What? Why?"

"Dammit, Molly," he said, his voice serious and low. "It's just … the car."

"You're damn near crying because of that stupid car!"

"It wasn't stupid." He put his nose in the air. "It was a beautiful thing. And we killed it. Molly, we *killed* it."

I rolled my eyes. "Audrey told me they had more than enough insurance to cover the car."

"You can't just buy another James Bond car," he snapped, gesturing wildly. "There are a finite number of them in the world."

"You're a bit of a lunatic sometimes."

He glanced at his watch. "I have to go catch my flight now. It'll be good to get back to Scotland."

"Enjoy your endless rain." I stood up and got my suitcase off the floor.

Rhys squeezed my hand and kissed me. I had to admit it—his lips were very soft.

"I'm glad you have your freckles back, kid."

"You have to stop kissing me, okay?"

He stood up straight and grinned. "Only when you stop kissing me back." He grabbed his suitcase and strolled away to his departure gate, glancing at me over his shoulder before disappearing around a corner.

CHAPTER TWENTY

A bell above the door jingled as I walked into the pawnshop in Fairfield, Connecticut. A few people were milling around, looking at used guitars hanging on the walls and jewelry lined up in rows in display cabinets.

I examined a guitar mounted behind protective glass before returning to the cabinets, checking out the sparkly items within. The guy behind the counter smiled at me.

"Can I help you find something?"

"Yeah, maybe." I looked over my shoulder. "I'm looking for some old jewelry. Real diamonds."

He raised an eyebrow. "I assure you, we don't purchase jewelry with fake gems."

"Except that one." I pointed to a diamond-encrusted brooch on a pillow and then to a nearby ring. "And that one. And everything else in this cabinet."

His eyes widened. "Ma'am. Those are all *real*—"

"No, they're not and we both know it." I made sure to

keep my voice low and my demeanor calm. "Now. I'd like to see the good stuff. Do you understand?"

He glanced around at the other patrons and nodded. "I keep them in my office."

He looked annoyed. I guess I would be annoyed too if a twenty-something in jeans and a hoodie came strolling into my store and knew immediately which items were bogus.

I followed him to a small room in the back. He closed the door behind me, glancing at me nervously.

He unlocked a safe and took out several flat boxes. He lifted off the covers. I certainly had a lot of different styles and colors to choose from. Rings, necklaces, brooches and bracelets—all real gems. Bands of silver, gold and platinum.

"How ... how did you know ... about our other selection?"

"Calm down," I said, not looking away from the lovely pieces on the desk in front of me. "I'm not going to report you."

I picked up a diamond necklace with a teardrop emerald hanging from it.

"That one's beautiful." The man nodded. "Just got that one in a few days ago."

I nodded. "It's nice." I put it back down and inspected a diamond ring. It was a round diamond with little silver pieces surrounding it, making the setting look like a glittery lotus flower. Written in tiny letters inside the silver band were the words 'I will love you forever.'

I quickly surveyed the rest of the pieces before turning to face the salesman.

"I'll take this ring and the necklace."

He frowned at me. "You don't even know how

much they cost."

I batted my eyelashes innocently. "I assume you'll give me a fair price, especially since every piece of jewelry you have out there is fake. Plus, you've got that fake 1965 Fender Stratocaster out there—"

He crossed his arms over his chest. "The Strat is *not* a fake! We got it from a trusted seller. He wouldn't screw us like that."

I shrugged. "Don't shoot the messenger."

His right eye twitched as he considered this. He breathed out slowly, closed his eyes and cleared his throat. He looked like he might be sick.

"Will that be cash or credit, ma'am?"

* * *

"And who are you?"

"I'm his daughter."

"Oh," the nurse said, peering at me over the top of his clipboard. "Paul didn't mention he had a daughter." Lines appeared at the corner of her mouth as she smiled. "Go on in."

I nodded my thanks. The police officer stationed outside the door didn't even glance at me as I slipped into the private hospital room. Paul, sitting up in bed while reading a newspaper, looked up and glanced nervously at the security guard.

"Good morning, young lady. Didn't expect to see you here … today."

"Hi, Dad."

Paul rolled his eyes and I sat beside him on the hospital

bed. He glanced at the guard outside and lowered his voice. "You shouldn't be here."

"It's okay. I wanted to see you. How are you?"

Paul smiled and patted his bandaged chest. "I've been better. The doctors say I'm lucky. God was looking out for me that day."

I glanced at the doorway. The cop was flirting with a pretty nurse.

"Everything's going to be okay," I whispered. "You're safe now."

Paul rolled his eyes. "With that guy at my doorway? I doubt it."

"No, I mean it." I widened my eyes so he would catch my drift. "*You're safe now.*"

Paul sat back on his pillow and nodded. "Is that so?"

"Yup. I'll tell you about it later when you're out."

A vase of flowers sat on the windowsill. The edges of the petals looked a bit wrinkled and faded.

"My son's girlfriend brought me those a few days ago." He chuckled and winced, rubbing his chest again. "I told her to bring a pizza next time!"

I laughed and adjusted my wig. "I should probably go. Can I get you anything? A soda? Something from the cafeteria maybe?"

"I'm fine. I'm glad you stopped by." He smiled and held my hand. "You take care of yourself, missy."

"I always do."

* * *

I pulled a blanket around my feet while reading a book on the sofa. The sun was shining in, making me all warm and sleepy.

The intercom buzzed. I reluctantly left my perfect place on the sofa and answered it.

"Housekeeping!" I sang into the intercom. The intercom crackled a bit in reply.

"Oh. I'm sorry." It was Nate. "Did Molly get a housekeeper?"

I laughed. "It's me. I'm just kidding. Come on up."

I was expecting him to call or text me, but for him to actually show up at my apartment was a nice gesture. I quickly ran to the bathroom to check my hair and make sure I didn't look like a total slob before answering the door.

Nate arrived at the door and I let him in with a smile.

"Can I get you a bottle of water or anything?" I asked. "Maybe a beer?"

He rubbed his shoulder awkwardly. "No, that's alright." He forced himself to make eye contact. "Thanks, though."

I nodded. "How are you?"

"A little confused." He leaned against the wall, his hands stuffed into the pockets of his jeans.

"Oh?" I got a bottle of water out and twisted off the cap.

"Yeah. I got a call from my grandmother this morning."

I sat cross-legged on the sofa and nodded. "How is she doing?"

"Her faith in humanity has been restored."

"What do you mean?"

"Burglars broke into her home and stole her TV and some jewelry that my grandfather gave her."

I sipped my water. "I'm sorry to hear that."

Nate gave me a look. "Do you find it odd that the burglars returned the jewelry to her by slipping an envelope under the front door? And that they also had a newer, bigger TV delivered to her?"

I shrugged. "They must have felt *really* bad."

Nate rolled his eyes. "Molly, I *know* that was you. I take it Ruby told you about the burglary?"

I smiled. "You can't prove anything."

He sat next to me on the sofa. "How did you get the jewelry back?"

"I went to every pawn shop in Bridgeport. Found the diamond tennis bracelet. Then I went to several pawn shops in Fairfield and found the ring and the necklace."

"Did you … steal them from the pawn shop?" He frowned.

"No," I snapped. "I bought them."

"Oh." He stared at me for a moment while he figured out what to say. "Why did you do that?"

"Because you love your grandma," I said. "And people who steal from seniors living on a pension piss me off."

Nate slid his hand into mine and held it. "It was a very nice thing to do."

"I felt like I probably owed you after all the shitty things I've said and done—"

"No, I was the one who was being shitty," he said. "Your job … what you do … it still scares the hell out of me, honestly." Nate smiled shyly. He really was a lovely guy. "But I still feel … the same way I felt before, about you." His soft thumb brushed mine as he held my hand. "I don't know what to do about that."

I just wanted to hug him *so much*. But I didn't.

"I'd like to try again," he said. "We can make it work."

I slid my hand away from his. "I don't think so."

He raised his eyebrows. "What?"

My stomach turned. It would be much easier if Nate could just read my mind instead of me having to actually utter the words.

"I'm never going to be able to make you happy," I said, avoiding his eyes. "I'm not about to give up what I do. It's not just a job to me. You're never going to be okay with it and you know it. You *shouldn't* be okay with it. If you *were* okay with it, you wouldn't be who you are."

Nate stared at me, bewilderment painted on his face. "Uh … okay." He sat back on the sofa and stared at the ceiling. "That's not what I was expecting you to say."

"I'm sorry. I just don't think we're a good fit. I care about you a lot. I'd love it if we could stay friends." A wave of relief washed over me. There. I said it.

"I thought I might even be moving back in with you."

I shook my head. "I'm actually selling this place and moving next month."

"What? Why?"

"Because I don't need a two-bedroom condo this close to the park," I said. "I'm gone more than I'm here. It just doesn't make sense."

What I didn't tell Nate was my plan to donate every penny from the sale of the apartment to a women's shelter in Brooklyn. The idea came from Ruby. To date, it's the smartest thing she's ever said.

Nate and I hugged goodbye and he left. I could tell he

was hurt and confused. But he was a catch. Any woman would be lucky to have him. That woman just wasn't me.

I went back to the sunny spot on the sofa and stared out the window. More than anything else about this apartment, I'd miss the view.

Maybe I'll keep a key to this apartment so I can occasionally check up on it, just in case.

I opened my book once more but was soon interrupted by my phone. I answered it.

"Oh, good. For once, you're not sleeping."

"Hi, Audrey." I smiled. "How are things?"

"No time to chat. I have to ask you something."

I sat up. "Yes?"

"Have you ever been to Barcelona?"

I thought for a moment.

That's in South America, right?

THANK YOU FOR READING

Thank you so much for reading
Molly Miranda: Thief for Hire.

If you enjoyed this book, please consider leaving a review
on Amazon, Goodreads, iBooks or the inside of a sketchy
bathroom stall. Ya know, wherever. I would appreciate it.
Your positive vibes would really help me out.

If you'd like to get an email notification when the sequel
is released, you can sign up for my mailing list at:

www.Jillianne-Hamilton.com/enews

ACKNOWLEDGEMENTS

Major kudos to my editors Colleen McKie and Allister Thompson. Thank you to Patti Larsen for her words of wisdom and K.M. Weiland for her book *Outlining Your Novel: Map Your Way to Success*—it saved me.

Thank you to all the English teachers I had in school who encouraged me to write.

Thanks to Louise Rennison and Meg Cabot for inspiring me.

I'd also like to thank:
Ashley Paynter, Melissa McInnis, April Condon, Jessica Caseley, Leo McKay and Bronwen Breeze.
Thank you for believing in me.

Thank you to former jewel thief Bill Mason.
Bill, if you ever happen to read this, can you please contact me? I'd love to chat.

ABOUT THE AUTHOR

Jillianne Hamilton is a writer and graphic designer. She studied Journalism and Interactive Multimedia in college and her writing has been published in *The Truro Daily News*, *The Sackville Tribune-Post*, *Macleans OnCampus* and the *PEI Writes 2013 Anthology*. She grew up in Nova Scotia and now lives in Charlottetown, Prince Edward Island on Canada's east coast. She enjoys corgi GIF animations and chocolate cheese cake.

www.JillianneHamilton.com
www.twitter.com/JillianneWrites
www.facebook.com/JillianneHamilton

Made in the USA
San Bernardino, CA
15 August 2019